FALSE
TRUTH

FALSE TRUTH

C.D. STEELE

The Book Guild Ltd

First published in Great Britain in 2021 by
The Book Guild Ltd
9 Priory Business Park
Wistow Road, Kibworth
Leicestershire, LE8 0RX
Freephone: 0800 999 2982
www.bookguild.co.uk
Email: info@bookguild.co.uk
Twitter: @bookguild

This work is entirely fictitious and bears no resemblance to any persons living or dead.

Typeset in 11pt Minion Pro

Printed and bound in the UK by TJ Books LTD, Padstow, Cornwall

ISBN 978 1913551 735

British Library Cataloguing in Publication Data.
A catalogue record for this book is available from the British Library.

In memory of my grandfather Harry McCullough

PROLOGUE

"**G**OAL! WHAT A FINISH, THAT NOW MAKES IT TWO-nil to Northampton – surely there is no way back now for Leyton Orient?" the TV commentary blared out from the live-stream.

"Bloody useless," shouted Liam Devlin as he ran into the living room from the kitchen. "We will get relegated at this rate." Liam, of course, would have been playing for his beloved Leyton Orient tonight had he not currently been serving a twelve-match ban for illegal betting. The urge had been there tonight, just as the urge was always there, to place a bet on pretty much any football match, or any sport for that matter. Had he placed a bet tonight it would have been against his own team, as their win record without him in the team was nothing short of abysmal.

Liam Devlin was Leyton Orient's star striker; he was top scorer for them last season when they surprised many by sneaking into the play-offs. He made his debut at the age of sixteen three years ago and had represented his country at every level from schoolboys through to the England U21 team, where he was earning rave reviews and was being scouted by numerous Premier League clubs up until his recent ban.

He cracked the ring pull on another can of lager, his sixth of the evening, and sat down on his leather sofa, depressed. Liam had suffered with depression on/off since the age of thirteen and nothing depressed him more than not being able to play football. He disconnected his laptop from his TV; he couldn't bear to watch any more of the match. Suddenly there was a knock at the front door of his apartment. He considered getting up to answer the door, but only for a second; he didn't have the energy and he wasn't in the mood for people right now. He turned his phone off and just sat there in the dark.

ONE

HE CAUGHT A GLIMPSE OF THE MAN THROUGH HIS camera lens; he was coming out of an apartment block carrying a leather-look briefcase. He was talking on his phone; a minute or two later a long-legged blonde-haired woman in her thirties came out after him. The man ended the call and turned to face the woman; they exchanged a few words, then all of a sudden embraced and kissed each other passionately. "Bingo!" Joe Wilde said to himself as he repeatedly snapped the unsuspecting couple. After about thirty seconds the couple unclenched, the man walked over and got into his silver Mercedes while the woman got into a blue Volkswagen Polo. They exited the car park, driving off in separate directions.

Work for Joe Wilde was currently very slow, as it had been pretty much for the past six months. This was one job out of just two he had on at the moment – a real contrast to his previous and only other proper job

1

working for MI6. Even when there was a steady stream of cases it consisted mainly of tailing different husbands whose wives suspected they were having an affair. The majority of the time it wasn't so much to confirm their worst fear, that the love of their life was cheating, or for reassurance they were barking up the wrong tree, but more looking for concrete proof so they would have grounds for divorce and to screw the bastard for as much money as they could. Joe often got the feeling that most of these women were in fact hoping their husbands were actually having an affair. This work was a far cry from the exotic world of international espionage.

It was nearly noon and Joe was due to meet up with a friend and former work colleague, Phil Harkes, for lunch. They first met at Fort Monkton in Portsmouth where they learnt advanced field training tactics and worked together for over ten years in MI6. Phil was now working for MI5 in counter-terrorism – or T branch, as it is otherwise known – which he transferred to five years ago. They met up for lunch a couple of times a month, usually at the small bistro just round the corner from Joe's office. Joe put his car in gear and started making his way to the bistro.

When he arrived he could see Phil already sitting down in a booth at the far right corner looking at his phone. Phil was five foot ten, of stocky build with thinning dark brown hair, whereas Joe was over six foot with an athletic build and had thick, wavy dirty blond hair. They were both forty-one years of age, although Phil looked as if he was at least ten years older, which Joe was never slow to remind him of.

"Alright, Phil, not like you to be early."

"I am on a tight schedule today, mate. I have already ordered for both of us."

"Oh, right, so nothing to do with the fact it is my turn to pay then, is it?"

"Don't worry, I haven't gone overboard. I know how tight you are."

"Behave, you know I am not tight. It's just that unlike you, I haven't got a regular income to rely on."

"Things haven't picked up for you yet then?"

"If anything it's getting worse. I could do with something big and time-consuming so I can rack up the hourly billing, even if it is just boring stakeout work. Anyway, what's the rush? I thought things were beginning to calm down a bit for you guys now after the death of that MP."

The MP in question was a certain Malcolm Walcott, who had been a member of the Tory cabinet as Minister for Education, a real hot-shot and rising star who had been hotly tipped to become Prime Minister one day. He was caught in a bomb blast eight weeks ago, along with two other MPs, and died instantly. The other two MPs survived but sustained serious injuries. Two members of the public were also killed in the blast, while another twenty were injured. The attack was carried out by a far-right extremist group called the National League. Malcolm Walcott was of West Indian descent and one of the other MPs, a Khalid Mahmood, was Muslim. Robin Griffiths, the notorious leader of the National League, was arrested for carrying out the bombing; however, he was murdered by Islamic converts inside prison when on remand awaiting trial.

3

"That's the thing, Joe, we have received strong intel that the National League has been planning another attack and is due to strike any day now, so it's all hands on deck – obviously I can't say much more than that."

"You think they are going to try and take out another prominent MP?"

"Highly unlikely – security rou the Cabinet and Shadow Cabinet has been increased tenfold, especially in and around Westminster, since the last attack. Ethnic minorities will obviously be the target – it's just a case of who exactly and when."

"I get the feeling you know more than you are letting on, Phil, but I know I am no longer privy to such information and won't push you for more."

Phil just gave a slight nod at this but didn't say anything else.

TWO

"**H**I, JACKIE, I AM BACK. ANYTHING COME IN?"

Joe asked more in hope than expectation. Jackie Wilkes had been his secretary for the past four years; he'd hired her a year after starting the business. She was sixty-one and widowed. She didn't have that many interests and seemed happy to come in earlier and stay later than her conditioned working hours. He found her to be very efficient and hard-working.

"Well, as a matter of fact, there is. I received a call from a woman called Sally Devlin – she stated she is the mother of Liam Devlin."

She waited for Joe to respond, but he just stared at her with a blank look on his face.

"Liam Devlin was the footballer who went missing about six weeks ago – you know, the story was all over the papers."

Joe was not a football fan, but he did vaguely

remember reading something about the disappearance of a footballer.

"Ah, yes, I remember now – suspected suicide. His car was found abandoned on Lea Bridge, but his body is yet to be recovered. Did she say what she wanted the services of a PI for?"

"She didn't go into much detail but said she believes her son is still alive. I have booked her in to see you first thing in the morning."

Joe didn't like the sound of this; it wasn't uncommon for family members – mothers especially – to refuse to accept that a loved one had passed on and would cling on to the slightest hope that they may still be alive. He didn't like the idea of chasing a ghost and charging someone for doing so, even if he was skint; it would feel like taking advantage of someone's grief. Joe sat down at his desk and opened his laptop to look up the details of the 'suspected suicide' online.

Liam Devlin's car was found abandoned on the Lea Bridge in Hackney, London, a local suicide hotspot. There were at least half a dozen empty cans of lager on the floor of his BMW, as well as a bottle of vodka that was two thirds empty. There were no witnesses who saw him drive to the location, let alone jump. The newspaper gave a detailed biography of Liam; it referenced that he had suffered severe bouts of depression for a number of years, and it also documented his well-known gambling problems.

At 9:00am the following day Jackie knocked on Joe's office door.

"Mrs Devlin is here to see you."

"Yes, no problem, send her in, Jackie."

A dark-haired woman entered his office; she was around five foot eight. Joe could see that she was a fairly attractive woman but looked very tired, with bags under her eyes; she clearly hadn't been sleeping well.

"Nice to meet you, Mrs Devlin, please take a seat. My secretary told me that you believe your son may still be alive – why do you think that might be?"

"I don't think, Mr Wilde, I know he is alive."

"OK, so have you seen him or spoken to him then?"

"No, nothing like that – just call it mother's intuition."

Joe had to try hard not to roll his eyes. "Look, Mrs Devlin, you have been through a terrible ordeal, but if you want me to investigate your son's disappearance, I am going to need something a bit more than mother's intuition to go on. It is perfectly natural for people who have lost a loved one to refuse to accept they may be gone, especially if the body is yet to be recovered."

"Don't patronise me, Mr Wilde," she said in a terse tone of voice. "Over the past fortnight I have been receiving calls late at night. Most of the time no one speaks, but I can hear gentle breathing and on two occasions someone quietly said, 'Mum,' in a muffled tone then hung up, and just a few days ago I received this in the post." She handed him a postcard which had scenes from Rio de Janeiro on the front, including Christ the Redeemer; on the back there was no writing, just the recipient postal address.

"So you believe this is from Liam? Mrs Devlin, I will try my best to not appear insensitive, but this postcard

7

and the phone calls you have received are more than likely the work of pranksters. There are some very sick individuals in the world who unfortunately get a real kick out of this sort of thing."

"Yes, I hear what you are saying, Mr Wilde, but I don't think so, and anyway, this is what I would like you to investigate. I have been led to believe you have had quite a bit of success in the past locating 'missing persons'. I know that the papers painted a picture of my son as some sort of manic depressive and alcoholic who couldn't control his gambling urges, but that was not who my son really was. Yes, he had his problems, like everyone, but the tabloids like to knock people down just as quickly as they build them up. My son was not a manic depressive; he was never diagnosed with such a condition. Yes, he suffered bouts of depression over the years, but he would snap out of them after a few days. He liked to have a drink, just like most young men of his age, but he certainly did not drink to excess – his career was far too important to him. As for the gambling, he was getting this under control; he was attending counselling sessions for it and had come to an agreement with the bookies over paying back the debt he owed them over a period of time. He loved playing football – it's what he lived for. It was only a matter of time before he moved to a Premier League club and started playing for his country at senior level. I just can't believe he would take his own life; he had far too much to live for."

She started to well up, so Joe offered her a tissue.

"Did you report the phone calls and the postcard you received to the police?"

"I did, yes, but they pretty much took the same view as you – that they were most likely pranks. Mr Wilde, if there is just the slightest chance that my Liam is still out there, I want to make sure I tried everything I could to try and find him. I wouldn't be able to live with myself otherwise."

THREE

JOE OPENED THE FRONT DOOR TO LIAM'S apartment using the set of keys Sally Devlin had given to him. According to her, the apartment had been a bit of a tip when she first went there after Liam's disappearance, but as he walked into the living room he could see that the apartment had obviously been cleaned and tidied by Sally Devlin. So any possible clues as to the disappearance of Liam could have been moved or removed altogether, although Joe was still firmly of the belief there was nothing suspicious in his disappearance and no doubt his body would be discovered sooner or later. He walked into Liam's bedroom, which was rather swanky and the bed was made up with silk sheets. There was a top-of-the-range Apple Macbook Pro sitting on a desk by a window. Joe walked over to it and booted up the laptop. It was password-protected, as he suspected it would be.

He called his friend Mark who used to work for MI6 as a technician and data analyst and was now retired. 'Hi, Mark, how's it—"

"Don't tell me, Joe, you want me to hack into someone's PC and their email account."

"How did you guess?"

"Oh, I must have psychic abilities. So who is it this time?"

"His name is, or was, Liam Devlin."

"Not that young footballer, is it?"

"Yes, one and the same."

"How come you are investigating him?"

"His mother has hired me to look into his disappearance."

"You think there might be foul play involved?"

"No idea yet, but I might have a better idea if you get me into his bloody laptop."

"Yes, sorry."

Joe gave Mark the MAC address of the laptop, as well as the internet router's IP address.

"Just give us a few minutes, Joe."

While Joe was waiting he took a look at some football trophies that were on display on a shelf in the bedroom. One in particular caught his eye, as it appeared to be broken. He took a closer look at it. Inscribed on the base were the words 'England U15 player of the year award 2015'. The trophy was of a player with a ball at his feet, but the player's left arm was missing; it looked like it had broken off at some point. He placed it back on the shelf.

"You should be able to get in now."

"Cheers, Mark, I owe you one."

"One! I have lost track of how many favours you owe me, Joe."

"You know I am good for it. I will catch you later, mate, cheers."

Joe decided to look at Liam's internet history first. The thing that struck him almost immediately was that the vast majority of the websites visited were either gambling sites or gay male porn websites. Joe thought back to the newspaper articles he had read online regarding Liam – none of them had mentioned he was gay, although they hadn't mentioned anything about girlfriends either, for that matter. Joe wondered if his family knew he was possibly gay – particularly his mother, as she hadn't mentioned it to him in their meeting, or maybe she just didn't believe it was relevant to her son's disappearance.

Joe then checked through Liam's emails. There was nothing much of interest sitting in the inbox, but when he checked the deleted emails folder he noticed there had been quite a few emails received from a John Wilcox in the two weeks leading up to Liam's disappearance. Joe opened up the earliest of these emails. From the opening paragraph it was quite obvious this John Wilcox was a former lover of Liam's due to the graphic sexual language used; it also seemed like John Wilcox was rather smitten with Liam. What was interesting, though, was Liam's reply to this first email. It read:

"John, as I have already told you, it is over between us. You need to stop contacting me – why do you think I never answer your phone calls or reply to your texts? You need to get over this and accept it for what it was:

just a fling. If you keep on trying to contact me and calling at my flat I will have no choice but to contact the police."

Joe read John's email reply to this:

"You don't mean this, Liam. I know you more than you know yourself. I know you love me – you are just scared of coming out, thinking it will have a negative impact on your career. It won't – you can be a role model for others like yourself in your profession. You can't live a lie all your life. I will not give up on you, Liam, ever. No one could ever love you the way I do – we are meant to be together."

It seems Liam did not respond to this email or to any of John's subsequent emails. However, as Joe continued to read the other emails it was clear that John Wilcox was getting frustrated that Liam would not reply; his emails became more angry and bitter, and the use of expletives became more frequent. When Joe got to the last email and read it, he almost broke out in a cold sweat.

FOUR

JOE PARKED HIS CAR OUTSIDE AN IMPRESSIVE mock-Tudor mansion in Walthamstow. This was where John Wilcox lived with his parents. He had obtained the address by looking up John's Facebook page. He got out of his car, walked up the gravel driveway to the front door and rang the doorbell. He was hoping that both of John's parents would be at work. According to John's Facebook page, he was enrolled on a business course at Waltham Forest College, but when he rang the college they advised him that John did not have any lectures that afternoon, so Joe thought there was a decent chance he would be at home. After about thirty seconds the door was opened by a young man who was about six foot tall, wearing skinny jeans. His hair was clearly dyed peroxide-blond and he wore diamond studs in both ears.

"Yes, how can I help you?"

"Hello, John Wilcox?"

"Yes, that's me, what do you want?"

"Hello, John, my name is Joe Wilde. I am a private investigator and I am currently investigating the disappearance of Liam Devlin. May I come in?"

"Erm, er, yes, I suppose so."

Joe was led into the kitchen.

"Take a seat, Mr Wilde."

"Thank you."

Joe took a seat and John sat opposite him on the other side of the kitchen table.

"I have been hired by Sally Devlin to investigate her son's disappearance."

"She thinks he may still be alive?" John asked.

"Yes, she does. What do you think, Mr Wilcox?"

"I honestly don't know. Without his body I guess there is always the hope that he may still be alive, but he was often depressed."

"Do you think he would be capable of taking his own life?"

"No, I don't think so, but then I didn't really know Liam all that well."

"Now now, Mr Wilcox, remember I am a private investigator – it is my job to delve deep into peoples' private lives. I know that you and Liam were in a sexual relationship for a while."

"OK, yes, but it was just sex. It wasn't anything deep and meaningful."

"Well, maybe that's how Liam viewed your relationship, but you certainly felt it was more than that. I have seen the emails you sent him."

John Wilcox looked dumbfounded by this revelation; he stammered slightly. "You... you have seen the emails?"

"Yes, including the very last email you sent him where you... let me just get this right."

Joe removed a print-out of the email from his jacket pocket. "Nobody has the right to treat me the way you have, Liam. I was there for you in your darkest moments, and I would always have been there for you because I love you, and this is how you repay me. Well, if I can't have you, then nobody can. I will kill you!" Joe let the words hang for a few seconds.

"I didn't kill him, I swear. I could never kill him; I was in love with him."

"And yet you threatened to kill him?"

"I was angry and hurt – I didn't mean it."

"Well, I suppose if the police had any evidence they would have charged you by now. No doubt you suffered some tough interrogation from them, though."

"The police never interrogated me; they never even paid me a visit."

Joe had to take a few seconds to take in what John Wilcox had just told him. "What, they didn't even question you?"

"No, I suppose they never saw those emails, and as far as I knew nobody was aware that Liam and I were seeing each other. Liam was afraid of coming out."

"So I have gathered."

Joe couldn't understand why the police had not taken in John Wilcox for questioning; by law they have the right to hack a missing person's email account for information, so they must have seen the emails. Joe decided he would need to speak to the senior investigating officer.

"So when was the last time you saw Liam in person before he disappeared?"

"It was the evening before I sent that first email. I went round his apartment about eight o'clock as we had agreed previously; that was when he told me it was all over between us."

"What was his frame of mind like when you last saw him? Did he seem depressed in any way?"

"No, not overly, but his mood could change very quickly from one week to the next. He was worried, though."

"Worried about what exactly?"

"The bookmakers he owed money to."

"I thought he had come to an agreement to pay back what he owed."

"No, not with all of them he hadn't. There was one in particular that he owed over fifteen grand to, a small, independent bookmaker."

"Was he not able to come to some agreement with them like he had with the others?"

"They weren't prepared to wait that long for their money. Liam said the owner and a couple of big men paid him a visit; they punched and kicked him then warned him if he didn't pay them back by the end of the month they would pay him another visit and he would suffer an even worse beating."

"When did this happen?"

"About two months ago."

"What is the name of the bookmakers?"

FIVE

"CAN I SPEAK TO THE DETECTIVE WHO IS IN charge of the Liam Devlin suspected suicide case, please?"

"May I have your name, please, and the reason you wish to speak with the lead detective regarding this case," the responder countered.

"My name is Joe Wilde, I am a private investigator and I have some information regarding the case."

"What kind of information, Mr Wilde?"

"I would prefer to only divulge this information to the detective in charge. Could I have his name, please?"

"Mr Wilde, you will need to tell me what you know otherwise I will not be able to put you through as the detective in charge is very busy and does not appreciate having his time wasted."

"OK then, it is regarding evidence of a threat made to Mr Devlin of which I believe the police would also have been aware of, and I have grave concerns as to how this case has been investigated. If I don't get speaking with the detective in charge I will have no option but to contact the police ombudsman service and make an official complaint."

"Hold the line, please, Mr Wilde."

Joe waited for about two minutes, listening to the inane hold music that was playing, until he was taken off hold and heard the same male voice again that he had just spoken to.

"The detective in charge of this case is a DI Whatmore. Unfortunately he is not able to take your call now, Mr Wilde, but if you give me your contact number I'll pass it on to him and he will call you back later on today, all being well."

Joe gave him his mobile telephone number before hanging up. He got up from his desk and headed out of the office door. "I am off to Hackney. I should be a couple of hours at the most, Jackie."

Joe had decided it was time to pay a visit to Parker's Bookmakers.

Joe stood outside Parker's Bookmakers; it was effectively just a small, dingy unit right beside a derelict old building that at one time had been a pub called the Nomads Inn. He walked through the frosted glass front door; there were about half a dozen punters inside watching various horse races that were showing live. A plump woman was manning the counter; he walked over to her.

"Are you wanting to place a bet, sir?"

"No, I would like to speak with the owner of this establishment, please."

"The owner is not here right now. To be honest, he very rarely comes in here – he is usually at one of the other businesses he runs."

"He has several businesses then?"

"He does; he is more often than not at Ritzy's, which is the nightclub he owns. It is not far from here."

She gave Joe the directions. Ritzy's nightclub was at the bottom of a narrow alley. Much like the bookies it wasn't much to look at; it looked like an old warehouse that had been converted. The name of the club was in neon lighting which wasn't currently turned on. Joe went up to the main door; there was an intercom on the wall next to it. He buzzed and waited for a response, a few seconds later a gruff voice came on asking him what he wanted.

"I would like to speak with the owner, please."

The owner in question was Frank Parker. While Joe had been walking to the club he used his phone to go on the internet to find out what he could about him. Frank Parker was originally from the East End of London; when in his teens and early twenties he had regularly been in trouble with the law. It was rumoured that he was employed by a notorious East End gangster back in the day. He was once arrested for stabbing a guy during a fight, but the charges were later dropped. As well as owning a bookmakers and Ritzy's nightclub, he also owned a couple of bars.

"And who are you?"

"My name is Joe Wilde, and I am a private investigator. I am investigating the disappearance of the footballer Liam Devlin."

"He is dead, isn't he – committed suicide?"

"Can't be certain of that."

"What has this got to do with Frank?"

"He knew him – Liam owed him money."

"Hold on a sec."

Joe was left waiting for a couple of minutes, before the gruff voice returned. "OK, Mr Wilde, you can come in."

There was a short buzzing noise then the sound of the door unlocking; Joe walked in.

"Follow me," the gruff voice said.

He was well over six feet tall, with a shaved head and all muscles – probably little brains. Joe followed him up a set of stairs. On the landing he stopped at the second door on the right and knocked.

"Come in."

They both entered a large dark office, with no windows; the only light emanating in the room was from a lamp sitting on a large desk. Sitting behind the desk was Frank Parker. He looked just like the pictures Joe had seen of him on the internet. He was fifty-six with thinning greyish hair, a large frame and a protruding belly. Unlike in the pictures, he was wearing reading glasses.

"Take a seat, Mr Wilde. I believe you are here about Liam Devlin, although I am not sure how I can help you."

"When was the last time you saw Liam, Mr Parker?"

"I have never met Liam Devlin."

"He owed you money, Mr Parker."

"Who told you that?"

"A little bird. It doesn't matter who told me – is it true?"

"Quite a few people owe me money, Mr Wilde."

"And was Liam one of them?"

"Not that it is really any of your business – yes, he did."

"Fifteen grand, right?"

"Thereabouts."

"But he wouldn't or couldn't pay you, isn't that right? I doubt you were too happy about this."

"Are you implying something, Mr Wilde?"

"No, not at all, Mr Parker, I am just trying to establish the facts. Do you normally let your punters run up such a tab?"

"Not normally, but Liam was a professional footballer."

"He was only playing for Leyton Orient in the fourth tier."

"Even players playing for lowly clubs often earn several grand a week, and don't forget that Liam was Orient's star player, so he would have almost certainly been the highest earner at the club."

"Did you threaten him if he didn't pay?"

"Not me personally, but I got a couple of my associates to call at his apartment and remind him of his obligation. They advised him that if he didn't pay up soon we would have no choice but to take out a judgement to have the debt enforced, which could lead to bailiff action."

"Is that all you threatened him with?"

"Yes, it was, Mr Wilde. What else could we threaten him with?"

"Oh, I don't know – what about violence?"

"I am a respectable businessman, Mr Wilde. I do not resort to tactics of violence and intimidation."

"That's not always been the case, though, has it, Mr Parker?"

"I don't care much for your tone, Mr Wilde. I didn't have to agree to see you and help with your enquiries."

"I have it on good authority that it was you who threatened Liam personally at his apartment. You probably took Brutas here with you." Joe nodded in the direction of the muscle-bound meathead who was standing behind him. "You roughed him up a little bit and warned him that if he didn't pay up in a couple of weeks you would pay him another visit. But this didn't have the desired effect, so I think you did pay him another visit and roughed him up even more. So what happened? You go too far and end up killing him? Dispose of his body then cover it up as a suicide?"

"I think this meeting is now over, Mr Wilde. You should be very careful when making accusations you can't substantiate. I do not have to answer your questions; you are not the police. What would I have to gain from killing him anyway? His debt would remain unpaid forever."

"Oh, I don't know – as a warning, perhaps, to others who owe you money, or maybe you went too far with the beating and ended up killing him accidentally."

"Show Mr Wilde out, please, Oliver."

The big brute walked over to Joe, but Joe got up before he reached him. "It's OK, I will show myself out."

Oliver walked close behind him anyway; he opened the door and Joe walked out. Just as he started walking in the direction of his car, his phone rang.

S I X

"HELLO."

"Hello, is that Mr Joe Wilde?"

"Yes, speaking, who is this?"

"This is Detective Inspector Carl Whatmore. I believe you wanted to speak to myself regarding the disappearance of Liam Devlin. Tell me, why are you so interested in this case?"

"I have been hired by Liam's mother Sally to investigate her son's disappearance. It appears she has lost confidence in the police and your investigation, and to be honest, I can't say I blame her, Detective."

"I did a bit of research on you, Mr Wilde, and I have also spoken to some of my colleagues who have worked with you in the past. It turns out you are very good at what you do – last year you managed to find two university students who had been missing for almost six months, tracked them down to some hippie commune in Indonesia as they wanted to live off-grid. However, there have been occasions when you have hindered police investigations, sometimes even withholding vital evidence. You like to do it all on your own, be the hero – perhaps it makes you feel more like you did when you were working for MI6."

"My only priority is to get results."

"I think we should meet, Mr Wilde. How about at that coffee shop just along from your office, say about seven?"

"Yes, fine, I will be there."

"That's good, see you then."

Joe hung up; he reached his car a minute or so later. Just as he was reaching into his pocket for the car keys, all of a sudden there was an almighty bang; it was deafening. Joe could feel the ground vibrate slightly as he put his hand to his ears. For a few seconds he couldn't hear anything, then he started to hear a faint ringing sound in his ears, or maybe it was just the numerous car alarms that had been set off by the explosion. It took a few more seconds for his senses to fully come back; he could just about make out people screaming and shouting. It seemed to be coming from a north-easterly direction. Joe started to run towards the commotion; as he was running the screaming was getting louder and louder. When he was about two blocks away from his car he turned right on to Well Street then stopped dead in his tracks; what he saw about two hundred yards in front of him was just utter devastation. It took Joe a few seconds to register what must have happened. It looked like a car had exploded right next to a mosque; there were people writing around on the floor screaming in agony and the wall of the mosque that was nearest the car had been almost totally destroyed. From what little he had seen already, most of the victims appeared to be Asian adults, but there were also some young children who must have also been caught in the blast. Some of the bodies on the ground were not moving at all. Joe wanted to help; he went over to the nearest body that was lying completely still. It was of a young Asian man in about his thirties. He was wearing a taqiyah cap and most of his clothes were covered in blood, as was quite a bit of the ground around him. Joe used his index and forefinger of his right hand to feel for the carotid artery to check for a pulse; the man's pulse was strong.

Just then a male paramedic ran up to Joe. "Step away, please, sir. I will handle this."

"He is not dead, there is a pulse."

"OK, good, don't worry, we have got this."

Joe looked around to see if there was anyone else he could provide assistance to; just as he started to walk towards another body, a police officer came running over to him.

"Please can you move away, sir, we are cordoning off this whole area."

"I am just wanting to help. I know CPR."

"It's OK, the emergency services are here – they can deal with this. We don't want any civilians in close proximity just in case there might be other bombs in the area that have yet to detonate."

Joe started to walk away. He was impressed by just how quickly the emergency services had responded to this incident; not just impressed – amazed, even. As he stood at the edge of the recently cordoned off area about 150 yards away from where the bomb had gone off, he looked around and saw other bystanders looking on, many of them recording the action on their mobile phones. Joe just walked away, gently shaking his head. He couldn't understand this modern phenomenon of people being fascinated by death and destruction.

SEVEN

JOE WALKED INTO THE RED BERRY CAFÉ AND looked around to check if he could see DI Whatmore. He knew what he looked like, as he had looked at photos of him from local newspaper articles online that covered crimes he had investigated. He was forty-eight years old with brown hair and a beard, around six foot tall with a slim build. He also had quite a prominent crooked nose. Joe couldn't see him, so he ordered himself a coffee then went to an empty table near a TV that was on in the corner of the room. He wanted to listen to a news report of the bomb attack he'd witnessed just a few hours earlier that was on. The report stated the mosque that had been targeted was Hackney Central Mosque on Well Street. The car bomb had exploded at 3:35; nine people had already been confirmed dead, five victims were in hospital in a critical condition and a further twelve picked up minor injuries in the blast. The National League were believed to have been responsible for the attack, although their spokesman had denied they were behind it. The reporter at the scene stated MI5 had gathered intelligence of an attack in Hackney but only at the eleventh hour and did not know the exact location. He praised the emergency services and stated the reason they were so quick on the scene was due to the intelligence MI5 had gathered, so they were on red alert for a terrorist attack in the area.

Joe was so engrossed in the news report that he didn't notice DI Whatmore walk in. The detective placed the coffee he had just bought, on the table and sat down opposite Joe. The detective's nose looked even more crooked in person and his beard had started to go grey in places.

"Terrible tragedy, that," he said, nodding towards the TV.

"I was actually there at the time."

"Seriously?"

"Well, I wasn't actually there when the bomb went off. I was a couple of blocks away, but I heard it and I witnessed the aftermath."

"Jesus, look, we can do this another time if you want."

"No, it's OK, I have witnessed worse."

"Course you have. What were you doing there exactly, following up a lead on Liam Devlin?"

"Maybe."

"Look, Mr Wilde, we are on the same side, you should tell me what you know and I will tell you what I know."

"Well, Liam's battle with depression is well documented, but in terms of suicide I just don't see it."

"You think he might have faked his own death?"

"No, I don't. He had received threats from two people just prior to his disappearance, at least one of which you should be aware of."

"I take it you are referring to John Wilcox."

"Yes, I paid him a visit and he said you never even questioned him about the threat."

"So because he said we didn't he must be telling the truth?"

"What would he have to gain by lying about that to me?"

"Who knows? People lie for all sorts of reasons. Look, Mr Wilde, there is absolutely no evidence of any foul play; forensics went over Liam's apartment and car with a fine-toothed comb. Obviously without his body the case cannot be closed, but taking everything into account the most probable outcome was suicide. Anyway, how did you know that John Wilcox had threatened Liam? I am sure as hell he didn't tell you, so I can only assume that you hacked into his email account, which, seeing as you aren't in the police, is actually illegal."

"Arrest me! I assume you don't know anything about Frank Parker."

"Who is he?"

"He was the other person to threaten Liam. He owns a bookies in Hackney and Liam owed him fifteen grand."

"I thought he had come to an agreement to pay back all his gambling debts?"

"Not with this one he hadn't."

"So did he threaten to kill him?"

"No, he didn't, but he paid Liam a visit a few months ago. He and a couple of his brutes gave him a bit of a beating and threatened him; they told him that if he didn't pay back what he owed soon they would be back in a few weeks and he would suffer an even more severe beating."

"And this Frank Parker told you this, did he?"

"No, it was John Wilcox who told me this."

DI Whatmore made a slightly sarcastic chuckle. "Ah, our friend John Wilcox again, who seems to be quite liberal with the truth. So did you confront this Frank Parker?"

"I did, yes. I went to see him at his nightclub, Ritzy's."

"And don't tell me, he denied everything."

"Well, of course, naturally."

"Naturally."

"The thing is, DI Whatmore, this Frank Parker has a police record and it is rumoured he used to work for a notorious East End gangster before moving to Hackney and setting up business. Also he once stabbed a guy, but the charges were later dropped for some mysterious reason."

"Where did you hear all this? Don't tell me, our friend Wilcox again."

"No, this information is in the public domain. I suggest you look into him."

"Are you trying to tell me how to do my job?"

"No, not at all, but maybe I should, as you don't seem to be very good at it!"

DI Whatmore gritted his teeth slightly and gave Joe what only could be described as a death stare. "Now, listen here, Mr Wilde, I know you think you are some kind of super sleuth, but I am an experienced detective and I have probably solved more cases and put away more dangerous criminals than you have had stakeout jobs. I don't have to indulge you and I am no longer going to. I urge you to stop looking into this case and leave it to the professionals. If you must insist on investigating this further, let me know anything you find out straight away, but don't get in our way or hinder the investigation because if you do I will have you arrested. Am I making myself clear, Mr Wilde?"

"Perfectly, Detective."

With that, DI Whatmore got up and walked out.

EIGHT

IT WAS AFTER NINE THE FOLLOWING MORNING, JOE
had scheduled an appointment for Sally Devlin to see
him for an update.

"I can't believe Joe didn't tell me he was homosexual."

"Did you never suspect at all?"

"No, the few relationships he had in the past were
with girls. They never lasted all that long as his football
career always took priority. Do you think this John
Wilcox did something to Liam?"

"It is a possibility, as unrequited love is a powerful
motive, but I think there's more chance of this Frank
Parker being responsible."

"He doesn't sound like a very pleasant man. If Liam
was so scared of what they might do to him, it would
explain why he faked his suicide and disappeared."

"It is a possibility, sure, but it would seem a bit
extreme. This Frank Parker character is a bit of thug, yes,

and I get the feeling he likes to throw his weight around and intimidate people, but it's not like he is a high-level organised crime lord, so Liam could have just gone to the police. I think it is more likely they paid him a second visit, perhaps went a bit too far with the beating and accidently killed him."

"Oh, God, but the police said they found no evidence of foul play."

"To be frank with you, Mrs Devlin, I have grave concerns over the way the police have handled the investigation into your son's disappearance. I would like to take another look at your son's apartment. I am also going to speak with the neighbours as well to see if they heard or saw anything in the days or even weeks leading up to Liam's disappearance."

Sally Devlin started sobbing; Joe got up and put his hand on her shoulder. "I will find out the truth about what happened to Liam, I promise, Mrs Devlin."

NINE

JOE ENTERED LIAM'S APARTMENT, THIS TIME equipped with a few tools such as a UV light to detect possible traces of blood not visible to the naked eye, a scraper, a few swabs and some polyurethane bags. Most of the apartment was painted in an off-white colour and the majority of the rooms had either light-coloured carpet or laminate flooring. This was fortunate, as using ultraviolet lighting to detect possible bloodstains only works on light-coloured surfaces. Bloodstains exposed to UV absorbs all light of that bandwidth so does not reflect back, therefore using it on dark surfaces would be pointless.

Joe started off in the living room. He went over the whole of the laminate floor, including the Persian rug under the modern marble coffee table in the middle of the room and the four walls. It took him over half an hour to go over the whole room, but he was only able to detect the odd tiny speck of blood that could easily have come from a simple nosebleed or tiny cut. He then moved into the bedroom to start the same process in there. Something about the room seemed different, but Joe couldn't put his finger on it. Just then there was a knock at the front door; Joe just waited for whoever it was to go away, but there was a second knock, then the doorbell was rung and then rung again – whoever it was, they were being persistent. Joe was careful that no one saw him enter the apartment, but he wasn't careful enough, it seemed. He reluctantly walked towards the door and opened it. A short elderly lady with permed grey hair stood before him.

"Hello, young man, I saw you enter young Mr Devlin's apartment nearly an hour ago. Can you tell me what you are doing?"

"My name is Joe; I am a friend of the family. Liam's mum Sally gave me a set of keys to his apartment as she wanted me to get a few things for her as she finds it too painful to come to this apartment herself."

Joe hoped that this nosey neighbour had not seen Sally Devlin enter the apartment since Liam's disappearance as he knew she had done so a couple of times.

"Of course, that's understandable. Sally is such a lovely woman; I met her on a couple of occasions when she called round to see her son. I feel so sorry for her; it's such a terrible thing to happen. Please give her my love – me and my family are praying for her."

"I will – sorry, what is your name, love?"

"Oh, God, do forgive me, I should have introduced myself. My name is Clara Worthington. I live in the ground-floor apartment on the opposite side of the road."

"Nice to meet you, Mrs Worthington. Tell me, did you know Liam well?"

"Oh, not really, I would often say hello whenever I saw him and he would sometimes stop and chat with me for a wee bit. I think he was just being polite – I mean, to young boys of his age I would just be some old fuddy-duddy."

"Did you ever meet any of his friends?"

"A couple, but we only exchanged hellos."

"Did you ever meet his friend John Wilcox?"

"I never caught their names, love."

"He was about six foot with bleach-blond hair and diamond earrings."

"Oh, yes, he was one of the two I met. He seemed very flash, although a bit odd as well."

"How do you mean odd?"

"Well, he would often call round to see Liam at all hours and sometimes he wouldn't even go into his apartment. He would just sit in his car at night for hours sometimes outside Liam's apartment. Then there were the terrible rows he and Liam had. I didn't hear them myself, but the Osborne's, who live in the apartment below, heard them – at one point they said they felt like calling the police."

"How many of these rows were there and when did they take place?"

"Not sure exactly – two or three. They happened… erm… now, let me think. I think they would have been some time in the two weeks before Liam's suicide."

"Possible suicide."

"Yes, of course, we pray that he will return safe and well. Well, I have probably taken up enough of your time;

I should let you get back to what you were doing. It was very nice to meet you, Joe."

"Yes, likewise, Clara – take care."

Joe closed the door and walked back towards the bedroom; after finishing in the apartment he would call on the Osborne's below. When he walked back through the door of the bedroom he suddenly noticed what was different about the room. The England U15 player of the year trophy that was slightly damaged was no longer sitting on the shelf with the rest of the trophies. Joe could only think that Sally Devlin had been back to the apartment and removed it, perhaps to take it to get repaired. The other thing he noticed was that the bed was probably a foot and half nearer to the left wall than it had been previously; he could see the marks on the carpet where the feet of the bed had been before it had been moved. Joe wondered if it had been moved to hide something, so he pushed the bed back to its original position.

He couldn't see anything immediately, but then when he inspected the carpet a little more closely he could see a faint stain of roughly a foot in diameter. Fortunately the carpet was beige, so Joe picked up the UV light, turned off the bedroom light and held it over the stain; it immediately picked up the presence of something that could well be blood. He put on a set of polythene gloves then started to pull away some carpet fibres from the stained area and put them in sealed polyurethane bag. After he had done this he resumed scanning the rest of the bedroom with the UV light. There was only one other area in the bedroom where there was the possible presence of blood and that was on the wall nearest the bloodstain where there was a noticeable splatter pattern that someone had tried to clean off, probably using bleach. Joe used his scraper to scrape away some of the blood-splatted paint into another bag. Once Joe had finished he then proceeded to do the en-suite bathroom, spare bedroom, toilet and kitchen, but he didn't find anything significant in these rooms.

T E N

JOE RANG THE DOORBELL AND WAITED; THERE were no lights on in the rooms on the side of the apartment he was facing. He waited for about thirty seconds then rang again; he waited for about another minute then turned to go and make his way down the external staircase to the ground floor, but just as he did so he heard the door unlock. He turned round to see a middle-aged man wearing striped pyjamas and a purple dressing gown.

"Oh, sorry. I didn't wake you up, did I?"

"No, no, we hadn't gone to bed yet. I was in the toilet when you rang and my wife must have fallen asleep watching the TV. How can I help you?"

"Hi there, my name is Joe Wilde." Joe didn't think there was much reason to lie about who he was this time. "I am a private investigator and I have been hired by Mrs Devlin to investigate her son's disappearance. I just wanted a few moments of your time, if I may, to ask you about anything you may have witnessed in the days and weeks leading up to Liam's disappearance."

"Forgive me, but at this time of night I am rather reluctant to invite strangers into my home."

"I quite understand, Mr Osborne. I can give you my card and you could call into my office when convenient instead if you like." Joe passed him his business card.

"How do you know my name, Mr Wilde?"

"Mrs Devlin told me."

"Ah, of course. Well, you do seem like a trustworthy person, so I suppose you can come on in. Would you like a cup of coffee, Mr Wilde?"

"Oh, I don't want you to go to any trouble."

"No trouble at all; the kettle is already boiled. I was just about to make one for myself and my wife – how do you take it?"

"White no sugar, thanks."

He poured the coffee and milk then handed one to Joe. "Follow me."

Joe followed him down the hallway and into the living room.

"Christine, we have a guest."

His wife, who was sitting at the far end of a plush three-piece suite, stirred from her sleep with a murmur then slowly opened her eyes. She was a middle-aged woman, probably in her late forties or early fifties, who was petite with short brown hair.

"Oh, my goodness! Who is this?"

"This is Mr Joe Wilde; he is a private detective."

"A private detective!"

"Yes, he is investigating the disappearance of young Liam."

"Oh, I see, do forgive me, Mr Wilde, I must have dozed off there."

"No need to apologise, Mrs Osborne. I won't take up too much of your time; I just want to ask you a few questions."

"Yes, that's fine. Please, call me Christine."

"Christine, did you or your husband see or hear anything unusual in the days or weeks before Liam's disappearance?"

"Well, apart from a few arguments – one in particular was very loud and aggressive and at one point we considered calling the police, didn't we, Clive?"

"Yes, that's right. He seemed to be arguing with a boyfriend, or possibly ex-boyfriend."

"Were you aware that Liam was gay and had a boyfriend?"

"No, we didn't until that last argument – from what we heard that night it was obvious he was," Christine replied.

"When did this particular argument take place?"

"The night before his car was found, wasn't it, Christine? Unless my memory is letting me down."

"No, you are right, Clive, it was, definitely."

"What! Are you sure?"

"Yes, absolutely."

"Am I correct in assuming the police never called to question you during their initial enquiries?"

"No, they didn't. We kept expecting them to call at some point, but they never did."

"Did you not think about contacting the police yourselves about giving them a statement regarding what you heard that night?"

"We did consider it, didn't we, Christine? But then we read in the local paper less than a week after Liam's disappearance that the police were not treating his disappearance as suspicious as there was no evidence of foul play."

"So can you tell me exactly what you heard that night? Mr Osborne, you go first."

"Well, it must have been around 9pm when we first heard raised voices coming from his apartment. Only slightly raised to begin with, but the argument got more and more heated. Liam was telling this guy John that he needed to accept that it was over between them and that he was getting on like a stalker. Liam must have given this guy John a set of keys to his apartment as he was demanding that he give them back, but he was refusing to do so. This John accused Liam of using him and said if he didn't take him back he would regret it. He threatened to go to the press and let them know that Liam was a homosexual and tell them all about their relationship."

"How did Liam respond to this?"

"He said that if John did that he would deny everything; he would get his locks changed and if John came round again he would call the police and tell them about the time John hit him and he had to go to hospital to get stitches."

"But this John character didn't seem perturbed by this," Christine interjected. "He said Liam wouldn't dare – it was just an empty threat as Liam would be too worried that if he told the police about their relationship it could be made public."

"The next thing we could make out was that Liam must have grabbed hold of this John fella as he started shouting, 'Get off me, Liam, get off me,' a couple of times, then it all went quiet," added Clive.

"How long did it stay quiet after that?"

"For the rest of the night. We didn't hear a thing from his apartment after that, did we, Clive?"

"No, to be honest, in hindsight I wish we had gone up and checked everything was alright."

"I am sure, but you shouldn't blame yourselves. Nobody would have imagined that Liam would suddenly go missing the very next day. Well, thank you for your time, Mr and Mrs Osborne, and for the cup of coffee."

"Not at all. I will show you out, Mr Wilde."

He and Clive walked towards the front door.

"Do you think this John character could have harmed Liam, maybe even killed him?"

"I honestly don't know, Mr Osborne, but I will need to speak with John Wilcox again very urgently."

ELEVEN

THE FOLLOWING MORNING JOE MADE HIS WAY BY
car to Walthamstow; he was hoping that John
Wilcox didn't have any lectures this morning. Joe still
wasn't sure about John Wilcox being involved in Liam's
disappearance, but he sure as hell had some explaining
to do. As he pulled into Tudor Drive he immediately
saw John's yellow Honda sports coupe travelling in the
opposite direction. It didn't look as if he had noticed Joe
as he drove past. Joe travelled on for another few hundred
yards before doing a quick U-turn and started following
him; he held back far enough so as not to make it obvious
he was tailing him. He followed him for a couple of miles
before he turned into Waltham Forest College car park.

Joe quickly parked his car then waited for John to
get out and start walking towards the front entrance of
the college. It appeared that John was in no rush to get
out; Joe assumed he must be on his phone or listening

to the radio, so he just waited. Joe had been waiting five minutes when he decided he had waited long enough and he would just go up and knock on his window. Just as he was about to open the door to get out he saw a man who was carrying something wrapped in a plastic carrier bag walk over to John's car, open the passenger door and get in. Joe waited again; just a couple of minutes later the man got out of John's car, but he no longer had the package with him. Joe took a good look at him; he was too old to be a student, unless, of course, he was a mature student. He was probably in his mid-thirties with longish jet-black hair and stubble. Joe could just about make out some tattoos on his left arm. Joe watched to see if this man headed towards the college entrance, but he didn't; he walked to the other side of the car park and got into a BMW which had a good few dents and drove off. Joe turned back to see that John had got out of his car and was walking towards the front door. Joe got out of his car and started briskly walking towards John in order to intercept him before he got inside.

"John, hold up!" Joe shouted.

John turned around; when he saw who it was he was slightly startled. He contemplated just ignoring Joe and heading on in but decided against it as he believed Joe would probably follow him inside anyway and he didn't want to create a scene inside the college.

"What do you want?"

"You lied to me about when you last saw Liam."

"Keep your voice down, will you? Let's move further away from the entrance."

John gestured towards the car park and they both started walking in that direction. They came to a bench.

"Shall we sit here?" Joe asked.

"Sure."

"I know that you saw Liam the evening before he disappeared."

"How do you know that?"

"It doesn't matter how. There is no point in lying to me, John, I will find out the truth eventually – it's what I do – so from now you are going to tell me the truth, OK?"

"OK," John replied sheepishly.

"Tell me what happened the last time you saw Liam."

"We rowed. When he stopped replying to my calls and texts I decided to call round – I thought that if I could see him in person again I could persuade him to keep our relationship going."

"Persuade or blackmail? You threatened to go to the press and let them know that Liam was a homosexual and tell them all about your relationship."

"Did someone overhear us arguing?"

"According to witnesses I am surprised the whole street didn't hear you."

"I wouldn't have done it; I was angry and hurt. When he refused to take me back I wanted him to suffer, to make him feel as bad as I felt, but he went mental. I had never seen him like that; he grabbed me by the throat and shoved me against the wall – he wouldn't let go. I was shouting at him to let me go, but he wouldn't, and his grip on my throat was getting tighter – I was scared."

"You feared for your life?"

"For a moment, yes."

"So what then? Did you lash out, grab something that was nearby and strike him with it?"

"No, no, I didn't, I swear!"

"It's OK, you feared for your life. It was self-defence – I am sure you didn't mean to kill him."

"No, I didn't, honestly, I swear nothing like that happened."

"You had a set of keys to Liam's apartment that you never gave back. You went to his apartment recently and removed that trophy from his bedroom, the one that was slightly damaged, didn't you? As this was what you struck him with!"

"Yes, I mean, no, I mean, yes, I did hit him with it, but not that night – it was a few weeks prior. I had my suspicions that he had been seeing someone else; he eventually admitted it and I just saw red. I picked up the trophy and struck him on the side of the head with it. I immediately regretted doing it. I couldn't believe what I had done. I mean, he wasn't knocked out or anything, but he was bleeding quite badly and was becoming groggy. I apologised and offered to take him to A&E to get it looked at, but he screamed at me to get out so I did. I texted him a couple of days later to see how he was and apologise. He seemed to have calmed down a bit; he replied saying he got a taxi to A&E later that night and they stitched up his wound. I was worried he might go to the police, but he said he just wanted to forget it."

"Oh, pull the other one. If this is really true, why did you enter his apartment recently and remove the trophy that you hit him with and move his bed to hide the bloodstain?"

"I was worried about how it would look, that's why. When you paid me a visit and said you were investigating Liam's disappearance, I panicked. I knew you had already been in Liam's apartment and that you may go back again, and I figured at some point you would question the neighbours. I was worried you would see the broken trophy and the bloodstain and assume that it might have been used as a murder weapon. That's why I took it, as it would have had my fingerprints on it. I also tried my best to remove the stain with some industrial stain remover, but it only worked a bit as the stain was still slightly visible. That's why I moved the bed to cover it, hoping you or anyone else wouldn't realise. I also hoped you hadn't noticed the trophy when you first went into Liam's apartment so wouldn't realise it had been taken, but obviously you must have seen it. This is the truth, you must believe me!"

Joe knew that he no longer needed to get the paint scrapings and carpet fibres analysed after what John had just told him.

"It really doesn't look good for you, John. Do you know what A&E Liam went to so I can try and corroborate all this?"

"I think it was Whipps Cross Hospital."

"Let's be clear on this, John. Even if I can get Liam's A&E appointment confirmed, that doesn't rule you out, as it won't prove what caused his head injury. Oh, and have you still got the trophy?"

"Yes, I haven't had time to dispose of it."

"Good, as you will need to give it to me."

"OK, I will bring it round to your office after my lectures have finished."

"No, you won't, John, we will go together to get it now!"

TWELVE

"SO WHAT DO YOU FANCY FOR LUNCH TODAY THEN, Phil?"

"Not sure, think I might go for fish cakes. What about yourself?"

"Think I will get the bacon and brie burger. Awful, that bombing at the mosque. You were so close to foiling their plot as well, it seems."

"Not close enough, I am afraid. The official death toll is now up to twelve, as three of the critically injured succumbed to their injuries. I can't believe you were there – lucky the nightclub that guy Parker owns wasn't on the same street as that bomb."

"Yeah, I suppose. Are you close to catching the National League members who were responsible?"

"Not yet, but we will. Anyway let's forget the National League – tell me all about this Liam Devlin case. Seems like you have finally got something to get your teeth into."

"Yeah, it makes a nice change."

"So you don't think it is suicide then?"

"Well, I am not ruling anything out. All I do know is that the police did not even attempt to conduct a proper investigation into his disappearance – it's almost like they want it to be an open-and-shut suicide case."

"Yes, that does seem a little odd, but then what with all the cutbacks the police have faced in recent years, perhaps we shouldn't be too surprised if some police forces are reluctant to throw resources at particular cases."

"Yeah, maybe," Joe muttered, but he wasn't convinced.

"Anyway, if they had conducted a proper investigation, there would have been no need for Sally Devlin to employ your services."

Joe chuckled. "Yes, very true."

A waitress came over to their table. "Are you ready to order, gentlemen?"

"Yes, I will have the fish cakes with chunky chips, please. Joe, have you decided?"

"Yes, the bacon and brie burger, also with chunky chips."

"Anything to drink?"

"Two sparkling mineral waters, please."

The waitress collected their menus and walked off.

"If it is murder, who is your money on Joe? John Wilcox or this Parker character?"

"Probably Frank Parker, but if he did kill him I don't believe it was intentional."

"You think it's more likely to be him despite the wealth of evidence against Wilcox?"

"Well, I went to Whipps Cross Hospital and they confirmed that they treated Liam Devlin on the evening of the ninth of January, 2020."

"But sure, that doesn't prove that he hit Liam with the trophy that particular night. Or maybe he used the same weapon twice? Just the second time it proved to be fatal."

"I just don't see it. I know jealousy can be a powerful motive and he has a bit of a temper, but he really was in love with Liam. I just can't see him as a killer."

"What about the threatening email he sent Liam?"

"He was angry – people often say things in the heat of the moment."

At that moment the waitress returned with their drinks. "There you go, gentlemen."

She turned to leave then suddenly turned round again. "I am sorry, but I couldn't help overhearing you talk about that footballer Liam Devlin – it's just that he came in here for lunch one day not all that long before he disappeared. I served him."

"You served him?" Joe replied. "When exactly was this?"

"Erm, let me think… it was the Tuesday before his disappearance."

"Was he with anyone?"

"No – he said he was waiting to meet someone, but they never showed up in the end."

"Did you talk much with him?"

"A good bit, yeah. You see, my brother is a massive O's fan. I knew he would be well jealous when I told him I got to chat with Liam, so I got him to sign his napkin."

"Did he say anything about the person he was supposed to meet?"

"No, just that it was a man."

"What did you speak to him about?"

"Well, it was mostly about the O's, a little bit of what he had been doing with himself during his twelve-match ban."

"What had he been doing?"

"Not much, really. He said he was finding it hard to fight the urge to gamble. I asked him if he had been to the bookies that day; he said he hadn't – he had been over at the internet café across the street before coming in here. He said his internet at home wasn't working. I asked why he didn't just use his phone to access the internet, but he said his phone wasn't working properly."

"What time did he come in here?"

"I would say it was about 12:30. I better go before my boss shouts at me as there are other people waiting to order. I will bring you your food when it is ready. My name is Danielle, by the way."

"OK, thanks, Danielle."

"No doubt you will be paying that internet café a visit after our lunch, Joe."

THIRTEEN

JOE WENT INTO THE INTERNET CAFÉ AND STRAIGHT up to the young woman who was behind the main counter.

"Good afternoon, could I please speak with the manager?"

"Can I not help you, sir?"

"No, I need to speak with the manager."

"Nothing's the matter, is it? Are you wanting to make a complaint?"

"No, nothing like that. I am a private detective and the manager may be able to assist me in an investigation." Joe showed the woman his card.

"Hold on, I will just get him." She walked through a staff door. A minute later she came out again with a man who was wearing a shirt and tie and looked to be in his thirties.

"Hello, my name is Jake, I am the manager of this café. How can I help you, sir?"

"Hi, Jake, my name is Joe Wilde and I am a private investigator."

"Yes, Amanda here just informed me. What is it I can do for you, Mr Wilde?"

"I am investigating the disappearance of the footballer Liam Devlin. I believe he came into this café on the twenty-eighth of January 2020, late morning, early afternoon, which was a few days before his supposed suicide. I need to know if you remember him being in here and if you spoke to him at all."

"Supposed suicide… I know his body has not been discovered, but you think that it could be something else?"

"That is what I am investigating. Do you remember him being in here?"

"No, I don't. I am not interested in football, so I wouldn't know him from Adam. I don't think Amanda would either."

Joe took out a photo of Liam and showed it to him. "Do you recognise him?"

"No, but I spend most of my time in the office out the back. Amanda or some of the other staff may remember him – Amanda, come here a sec."

"Yes, Jake."

"The guy in the photograph, he is the footballer Liam Devlin – you know, the one who was suspected of committing suicide a couple of months ago. Do you remember him being in here on the morning of the twenty-eighth of January 2020?"

"Erm, I don't think so. We get so many people coming in here. It's possible I could have served him, but I just don't remember, sorry. I will show it to Andrea and see if she remembers him."

"Thank you. Jake. I would like to go through your CCTV footage for that particular day if I may."

"Yeah, I suppose, sure."

"No, sorry, Mr Wilde, Andrea doesn't remember him either."

"OK, thanks anyway."

"Follow me, Mr Wilde, the CCTV hub is in my office."

Joe followed him out the back into a small office. Jake grabbed his swivel chair from behind his desk and pulled it towards a PC that was sitting on a desk against the back wall of the office.

"Grab a chair there, Joe, I will just get logged on here."

Joe sat beside Jake and watched him go into the archive CCTV file footage and search for the file dated the twenty-eighth of January 2020.

"Ah, here it is." He opened the file and the video started to load up. "What time would you like me to start from?"

"Try from 11:00."

"OK, this may sound like a stupid question, but what exactly are you looking for? I know you are checking to see if Liam came in that day, but so what if he did? How will that help you?"

"Well, if he did come in that day I am interested to see if he came in alone or with someone else, or if someone came in to meet him at some point."

Joe also wanted to see which computer terminal he used, but he wasn't going to tell the manager that, as at some point he was going to come back and get Mark to work his magic so he could see Liam's search history.

"We have two cameras out on the floor; they are video feeds B and C. Joe, you watch B, which covers the front of the café including the front door. I will watch C, which covers the back, just in case you miss him coming in."

They had got to twenty-three minutes past eleven on the recording when Joe saw a man who fitted Liam's description enter the café; the image of the video feed wasn't particularly clear, plus the video playback skipped a second at a time.

"Hey, I think I got him. Jake, rewind it a few seconds then zoom in on the front door."

They both watched intently as a young man walked in through the front door. Jake paused the video; the man was wearing a dark baseball cap.

"It's very difficult to tell – you think it's him, Mr Wilde?"

"Not one hundred per cent sure yet, but I am pretty confident that's him – let it play."

"I have some work to be getting on with, so I will just leave you to it, Mr Wilde."

"Yes, no problem, Jake, thanks."

Joe spent the next thirty-odd minutes watching who he now was certain was Liam. He watched him enter the café, order a coffee, then log in to a terminal near the back of the café. He was alone the whole time and didn't engage with any of the other customers or staff. However, he noticed there was something odd with his behaviour: he kept looking up and then over his shoulder every now and then, as if he was checking to make sure no one was watching him. Joe knew he definitely had to find out what Liam was looking at online that day.

FOURTEEN

IT WAS JUST AFTER MIDDAY THE FOLLOWING morning. Joe had originally planned to go back to the internet café and call his IT expert friend Mark when he got there, but he decided it would be best if he got Mark to go there instead, as he didn't want to raise any suspicions, even though the staff probably wouldn't have cared if he told them the reason. He had already given his friend Mark a heads-up regarding what he needed yesterday – namely searching for the archived temporary internet files from the date and time Liam accessed the internet on the particular terminal he used. He was just waiting for Mark to upload this data to a secured virtual save cloud from which he could access it and download it to his own computer. Just then he heard the front door open and someone start to make their way up the stairs. Suddenly his office door swung open.

"Hey there, Joe, mate, how's it going?"

"Phil! What an unpleasant surprise – what are you doing here?"

"Oh, you know, I happened to be in the area so I thought I would pop in and see you."

"Fair enough. I haven't got time to go for lunch today if that's what you were hoping."

"No, not at all, I wasn't planning on staying that long – a cuppa wouldn't go amiss though, old pal."

"Typical of you to call in when Jackie is out on her lunch, meaning I will have to make it. Make yourself comfortable for a few minutes while I go to the kitchen and make it. How are you taking it – the usual?"

"Yes, cheers, pal. So did Liam pay a visit to that internet café?" Phil said loud enough for Joe to hear him from the kitchen.

"Yes, he did. The manager allowed me to browse the CCTV footage; he was in there for an hour."

"Did he meet and speak to anyone while he was in there?"

"No, he spent the whole time on the internet. However he was acting quite oddly."

"In what way?"

"He would regularly look from side to side and over his shoulder as if he was checking that nobody was watching him."

"Have you found out what he was looking at online when he was in there?"

"Not yet, but I will. So the attack on the mosque – you definitely still think it was the National League who was behind it?"

"Why wouldn't we? All the intelligence we received

indicates it was, plus it fits their MO. Remember they attacked that mosque in Birmingham three years ago?"

"Yeah, I remember it, but they didn't use a car bomb that time; they just hurled a few Molotov cocktails, plus they keep denying responsibility for this one. Why take responsibility for the bombing that took the life of Malcolm Walcott but not this?"

"Who knows what their reason is. The IRA didn't always take responsibility for every bombing during their campaign of terror back in the '70s and '80s."

Joe walked into his office carrying two mugs of coffee and gave one to Phil. They spent another twenty minutes chatting mostly about old times when Joe's phone buzzed. He looked at it; it was a message from Mark, stating, "It's all there ready for you now." Joe replied with a simple, "Cheers."

"Well, I don't mean to be rude, old buddy – better be getting on with some work."

"Yes, no problem. I need to get going anyway, sure, keep me informed about how the case is going."

"Yes, will do."

Phil got up and walked out of the office and Joe accessed the secure cloud; he knew how to do this as Mark had previously saved stuff for him this way before and showed him how to access it. He started the process to download the files to his hard drive.

FIFTEEN

THE FOLLOWING MORNING JOE WAS WRITING UP his report on how the investigation was progressing, including yesterday's interesting findings from Liam's internet searches in preparation for his meeting with Sally Devlin that was arranged for 9am, which wasn't far off. He didn't have time to take on any more cases as the Liam Devlin case was taking up most of his time and now, with a very credible new lead, would likely take up even more of his time.

At 9:00 there was a knock on the door and Jackie let Sally Devlin into Joe's office.

"Good morning, Mrs Devlin, good to see you again. Please, take a seat."

"You said on the phone you had come across an interesting development, Mr Wilde."

"Yes, that's right, Mrs Devlin, I have discovered that on the twenty-eighth of January Liam spent a good hour in an internet café on Leyton High Road looking at websites such as Expatfinder and Escapeartist.com. He was looking up all you need to know before moving to Paraguay. Specifically the city of Asuncion in Paraguay, but he also looked up a website for information on a small town very close to Asuncion called Nanawa and a Facebook page dedicated to the town of Nanawa."

"You think that's where he could be? Oh my God, he is still alive. I knew it, but no one would listen to me."

"Hold on, Mrs Devlin, this is just speculation and is certainly worth investigating, but even if Liam did move to Paraguay, something may have happened to him since he moved. I mean, he didn't have much money left in his bank account – he may have had to sleep rough and could have been struggling for food. From what it appears, if he did move there it was a spur-of-the-moment decision, so I doubt he had time to learn Spanish."

"Spanish, but I thought you said he was searching online about living in Paraguay?"

"Spanish is the official language of Paraguay."

"Oh, I see. Tell me, Mr Wilde, is Paraguay near Brazil?"

"Yes, they border each other."

"So then that postcard I received probably was from him after all."

"Possibly, although that postcard was from Rio de Janeiro, which is still over a thousand miles away from Paraguay. It could still have been a prank. Just a bit of a coincidence, that's all."

"It was from him; I just know it was."

Joe could see a marked change in Sally Devlin; it was

like the weight of the world had suddenly been lifted from her shoulders.

"Obviously I would like to go over to this town of Nanawa."

"Yes, yes, you must, Mr Wilde," Sally Devlin interjected enthusiastically.

"There is the small matter of expense, though. I would probably need a week over there to conduct a thorough investigation, but obviously it is going to be a lot more expensive compared to doing a local investigation."

"Money is not a problem, Mr Wilde. After Liam disappeared my ex-husband, Liam's dad, set up a tribute page to Liam on Facebook with the option to make donations. A lot of people were very generous, God bless them. It was this money I used to hire you in the first place and there is still a good bit left."

"No problem, I will book the flight today. Hopefully I will be able to fly out tomorrow. Even if I do manage to find Liam, I can't promise that I will be able to persuade him to come back to the UK or even get him to contact you."

"I am not worried about that just yet – just so long as you find him and that I know he is safe and well will be more than enough to start with."

SIXTEEN

J OE WAS SITTING IN HIS SEAT WAITING FOR THE plane to take off. He had booked a seat in economy; even though Sally Devlin had stated that money wasn't an issue, he wasn't going to take advantage by flying first class and staying in luxury hotels. It was a twelve-hour flight to Paraguay and would give him plenty of time to read up on Asuncion, Nanawa and the local culture. He would also use this time to brush up on his Spanish. When working with MI6 he became fluent in several different languages including Spanish, but it had been a while since he had last spoken it.

The plane landed at the Silvio Pettirossi International Airport in Asuncion at 9:30pm local time. He was jet-lagged, as Paraguay is five hours behind UK time, and needed to get some sleep. He had tried to sleep on the plane without much success. When he had gone through passport control and customs he collected his luggage then headed to the front entrance to hail a cab. He had booked to stay at the Gran Hotel del Paraguay which was approximately 0.2 miles from Nanawa and was just over twenty-three miles from the airport. The taxi ride to the hotel would take approximately thirty-five minutes. Joe decided he would phone his mate Phil to tell him where he was, as he hadn't had a chance to contact him before he flew out. Phil answered almost immediately.

"Hi, Joe, what's up?"

"Hi, Phil, I am currently in Paraguay."

"What on earth are you doing over there?"

"Following up a lead on Liam Devlin, I discovered that Liam spent his time in the internet café looking at websites on all you need to know before moving to Paraguay. Specifically the city of Asuncion in Paraguay and also a small town very close to Asuncion called Nanawa. That is where I am travelling to right now, I have booked to stay in a hotel in Asuncion that is situated very close to Nanawa."

"Wow, so it is very possible that Liam is still alive then?"

"Yes, I believe so."

"If that is the case then he must have faked his suicide to flee to Paraguay – why on earth would he do that?"

"I have no idea, but I intend to find out."

"Do you think it might be because of Frank Parker?"

"It's a possibility, but even though he likes to use intimidation and menace, it is not like he is some big crime lord. Faking your own death to go and live in South America seems rather extreme just to escape someone who is no more than just a low-life thug. Surely you would just get the police involved."

"Unless the police are involved in his disappearance in some way – you already said that in your opinion they were reluctant to investigate Liam's disappearance properly."

"Maybe. Anyway, I am not sure how long I will be over here, but I will call you when I return home."

"Yes, no problem, mate. We can catch up when you return home. Good luck."

When they pulled up outside the hotel Joe paid the taxi driver his fare and got out, then the driver removed Joe's luggage from the boot and handed it to him. He then started walking towards the hotel entrance. The hotel was an old-style colonial hotel which had received loving restoration in order to maintain its historical heritage. The main building was surrounded by lush gardens with plenty of palm trees. Once he had checked in and was given his key card he headed up a couple of floors to his room. The room was comfortable and clean-looking, if not special, and had a small en-suite bathroom. He put his hold-all down on the bed and unpacked what little he had brought with him; he was hungry but was too tired to eat. After a quick shower he got into bed; he would walk into Nanawa early in the morning after some breakfast.

Joe left the hotel at 7:30 and started walking towards Nanawa; he had picked up a map of the local area from reception before leaving. The sky was overcast but the temperature was mild, which suited Joe as he wasn't overly fond of hot weather because he burnt really easily. As Joe crossed over to the other side of the street he noticed a tramp sitting on a bench in a very small park/botanical garden. Joe thought it would be a good idea to speak with him. If Liam had had to sleep rough after his money ran out then they may have got to know each other. Even if that wasn't the case, as the homeless generally move around a lot this guy may have seen Liam at some point. As Joe got closer to him he could see this guy was holding a bottle of something, probably a spirit of some kind, wrapped in a brown paper bag. He had long, greasy dark hair and a dark brown beard, which, on closer inspection, appeared to have some bits of food in it. As he stood in front of him Joe could make out the disgusting smell of stale urine on the guy's clothes.

"*Buenos dias,*" Joe said.

The man did not reply; he just took a swig while staring at the ground. Joe then asked him in Spanish if he knew a guy called Liam Devlin. The tramp shook his head and grunted, "No." Joe then asked him to look at a picture of Liam to see if he recognised him. The tramp looked at it for a few seconds then grunted, "No, sorry," in Spanish while gently shaking his head as he passed the photo back to Joe. The whole time he was stood there, the tramp did not make eye contact with him. Joe believed he was probably inebriated or he could just be a bit odd, as people in his position often were. Joe thanked him for his time and walked on.

It only took him just over five minutes to reach Nanawa. He wasn't able to find a great deal of information on the town of Nanawa other than that it was a town situated in the Presidente Hayes department of Paraguay. It had a population of just under seven thousand and the urban area was divided by the Pilcomayo River from the city of Clorinda in Argentina.

Joe decided he would start making enquiries in the local bars and restaurants. He had already asked numerous staff in the Gran Hotel del Paraguay if they knew of or had come across Liam on the off chance he had stayed or even worked there at some point, but no such luck. As he made his way to the town centre he came across a lively, bustling market that was taking place in the town square. Joe saw a bar on the left side of the square. "Good enough place as any to start," he thought to himself as he walked over to it. There were a few people sitting at tables on the outside of the bar; he greeted them then showed them the picture of Liam. None of them recognised Liam, so Joe went on inside. It was dark inside, as there were not many windows and only a couple of small lights. He went up to the barman and showed him the picture; a glimmer of recognition showed on his face, but the barman said he looked a little familiar but could not be sure.

Joe asked the rest of the staff and the few locals who were inside, but drew a blank. He next tried a bistro that was a couple of doors down from the bar, but with the same result. He then decided to ask a few of the market traders, but again, no luck, although he got the feeling they were too preoccupied in trying to sell their wares rather than help him and take a good look at the photograph of Liam.

It was almost noon and Joe was starting to feel hungry despite the fact he'd had a hearty breakfast; he put it down to all the nice smells emanating from the market. He went to the bistro he had been in earlier that morning and ordered some grilled sardines and chipa bread. Sitting at a table outside to wait on his order, he reflected on what had been a pretty fruitless morning; however, the barman's slight recognition had given him some hope.

After he finished his lunch Joe went back to the market and started questioning some of the locals who were doing their shopping; the vast majority he found very warm and friendly, but some of them didn't speak Spanish, just the indigenous language of Guarani, which Joe couldn't understand a word of. Most of the locals he spoke to did not recognise Liam; however, there were a couple who stated he looked vaguely familiar, but, like the barman, they could not be certain. Out of everyone he had spoken to that day, not one of them had come across the name Liam Devlin, so Joe suspected that if Liam was living here he was going by another name.

When Joe had finished in the market he made his way to the local church, which was open. The church was the Church of Jesus Christ of Latter-Day Saints; he walked through the main entrance of the church into the porch then on through to the nave. There were a few people sitting on the pews, some of which were praying; there was also an elderly lady cleaning the pews. Joe went up to her and showed her the photo of Liam and explained to her why he was looking for him. She didn't recognise him, so Joe then asked if the priest was around. She told him he was and asked Joe to follow her through a door that was behind and to the right of the pulpit. They walked down a corridor until they came to a door on their right. The lady knocked on the door and then opened it; a man who Joe presumed was the priest

– although he was dressed down and not in the usual priest regalia – turned around. The lady explained to him who Joe was and what he was doing here. The priest then shocked Joe slightly by greeting him in English.

"Nice to meet you. My name is Father Salvador Hernandez, and you are?"

"Father, my name is Joe Wilde. I am a private detective from England."

"Yes, Ramona was just telling me there," the priest responded as the elderly lady left the room. "I have not come across the name Liam Devlin, but let me have a look at the photograph, if I may."

"Your English is very good, Father."

"That's because I am actually Spanish and I learnt English when I was training to become a priest."

Joe handed the photograph to the priest. Father Hernandez appeared to be in his fifties, with a dark tan, as you'd expect from someone who lived in South America, with dark hair that was beginning to turn grey and a moustache.

He took a good long look at the photograph. "Well, I cannot say conclusively that I have seen this man, but about five weeks ago a young man came into this church – I would say he was in his late teens, early twenties, and what is more, he was English."

"English!" Joe's excitement suddenly grew.

"Yes."

"Did he look in any way like the guy in the photograph?"

"Well, it is hard to say, as this guy was wearing a baseball cap and sunglasses. He also had a beard."

"Did he speak with a Cockney accent?"

"Sorry, I don't know what Cockney is."

"It's the accent the vast majority of Londoners speak – that's where Liam was from, London."

"Ah, I see. I know my English is quite good, but I have never been to England, so I wouldn't know about accents."

"Did he say what he was doing here in Nanawa?"

"He said his name was Daniel and that he was on a gap year. He wanted to travel and see as much of the world as he could before starting university."

"Did he say what other countries he had been to? He didn't mention Brazil, by any chance?"

"Yes, he said Rio de Janeiro was one of the places he had been."

"Why did he come into the church?"

"He said he felt like praying even though he wasn't religious. He was worried about money as he didn't have much left and he needed to get a job of some kind and somewhere to stay."

"Did you give him any advice?"

"I suggested he try the hotels in Asuncion as they are always in need of staff such as waiters, bar stewards and cleaners, and they often provide accommodation instead of, or as well as pay. I also suggested he put his faith in God the almighty by praying more."

"He didn't mention anything about his life back in England, his family or anything like that?"

"No, nothing."

"What height would you say he was?"

"Oh, maybe about six foot, give or take. How tall is this Liam Devlin?"

"Six foot one, and what sort of beard did he have – long and bushy?"

"No, it wasn't. It looked just like a few days' growth – a week at the most, perhaps."

"So there is a good chance he is now working and living in Asuncion. God damn it, Asuncion is such a big city with numerous hotels."

Father Hernandez had a disapproving expression on his face and Joe suddenly realised why.

"Forgive me, Father, I didn't mean to take the Lord's name in vain."

"That's OK. I saw him again a week later walking in the market, so maybe he had managed to get a job here in Nanawa or with a hotel in Asuncion that is close to here."

"OK, well, thanks very much for your time, Father Hernandez, you have been very helpful."

"Not at all, Joe. I will pray that you are successful in finding him."

SEVENTEEN

THE FOLLOWING MORNING JOE SET OFF FROM HIS hotel to make his way into Asuncion. He needed to hire a car, but when he made enquiries at the hotel reception they advised him that there was nowhere in Nanawa to hire a car so he would need to go into Asuncion. Joe was going to spend the day going round all the hotels within a ten-mile radius of Nanawa. There was a hotel called the Premier Hill Suite Boutique just over a quarter of a mile away; he decided he would go there first on foot as it was close and on the way. As he walked away from the hotel he noticed the tramp he saw yesterday morning sitting at the same place; as he walked past him he threw some spare change into the cup the tramp had by his feet.

Joe arrived at the Premier Hill Suite Boutique Hotel less than ten minutes later. It was a slightly more modern hotel aimed at the budget market but still quite picturesque looking from the outside. He walked through the entrance into the main reception area. He went straight up to the reception desk and asked the lady who was on reception if it was possible to speak with the hotel manager. She asked Joe to wait a minute while she lifted up the phone and dialled the manager's office. After she put the phone down she informed Joe that the manager was on his way. Joe only had to wait a couple of minutes before the manager appeared. He had short hair with a side parting and wore glasses. He looked to be in his late thirties; the manager tag pinned to his suit had the name Alfredo de Menzez. Joe told him his name and asked him if he spoke English.

"A little bit," was the manager's reply.

"I am a private detective and I am trying to locate a missing person called Liam Devlin, although I believe he could be going by the name of Daniel – I don't know about the surname. I am going round all the local hotels, as I think he may have done the same thing trying to find employment."

"We had a young English man come here for employment a month ago. We took him on as a bar staff, and his name was Daniel – Daniel Walker."

Joe could barely contain himself. "This is excellent news. Is he working right now or even staying here?"

"No, he is not here."

"OK, when is his next shift?"

"No, you don't understand, Mr Wilde. When I say he is not here, I mean he does not work here anymore – he left just after one week."

"What! Did he find other employment? Did he tell you why he was leaving and where he was planning on going?"

"He said he needed to move on to find something that paid a bit better. The accommodation we provided here for him took most of his wages. He did mention that he was on a gap year travelling and was thinking about going to Bolivia next."

Joe couldn't believe it; just three weeks ago Liam was here in this very hotel. He was utterly deflated – so near and yet so far.

"Did he mention a particular town or city in Bolivia?"

"No, just Bolivia was all he said."

"If you don't mind, Mr de Menzez, I would like to question your staff. I would also like to take a look in the room he stayed in, just on the off chance he left something behind – a clue, perhaps, as to where he was thinking of going next."

"The room has been cleaned several times since he left, Mr Wilde. Even if he did leave something behind I doubt it would still be there."

"Even so, I would like to take a look all the same."

"Certainly, I will get you the key card."

Joe used the key card to unlock the door and walked into the small single room. The manager informed him the room had been unoccupied since Daniel/Liam left, which made it easier to look for clues. The room was plain and simple, with a single bed, one bedside table and a dresser along the opposite wall to the bed with a chair tucked under the middle of it. Joe immediately checked the drawers of the dresser, but there was nothing in them apart from a few old receipts. Next he tried the bedside table drawer. Again there was nothing much of interest – a few sweet wrappers, some more receipts – but just as Joe was about to close the drawer something caught his eye. At first glance he thought it was a photograph pressed up against the back wall of the drawer, but when he pulled it out he realised it was a postcard. It was a postcard of Asuncion. Joe's initial excitement was replaced with frustration; what he was really hoping to find was a map or travel guide of a particular town, city or district within Bolivia – if that was indeed where Liam had actually travelled on to. Joe searched the rest of the room, including the en-suite bathroom, checking under the bed, moving the furniture about to check if anything had fallen down the back, but he found nothing else.

Back in his hotel room, Joe was finishing off a meal. He had ordered room service rather than sit in the hotel restaurant, as he needed peace and quiet to think. He had to work on the assumption that Liam had gone to Bolivia like he told Alfredo de Menzez, as there were no other leads for him to go on. The trouble was that even though Bolivia is one of the smaller South American nations, it still has a population close to twelve million and there are over 1,300 towns and cities. Joe had to think of a way of narrowing his search. As Liam had been staying in Nanawa, a small town just outside the Paraguayan capital of Asuncion, Joe used his tablet to look up small towns similar in size to Nanawa that were located on the outskirts of Sucre, the capital of Bolivia. There were several; Joe believed he would have to visit them all, but goodness knows how long this would take. He would need to contact Sally Devlin and see if she had the funds to cover him staying there for a couple of weeks at the very least.

He started to take note of all the towns he planned to visit; there was one town that immediately stood out for no other reason than its name, Copacabana. The same name as the neighbourhood in Brazil made famous by the Barry Manilow song. Joe doubted very much the Bolivian Copacabana was anything like the one in Brazil.

After an hour of researching the various towns on the outskirts of Sucre he got himself ready for bed; as he got into bed he pulled up the bedsheets then leant across to turn off the bedside light. As he was doing so he glanced at the postcard of Asuncion that he had found in Liam's room at the hotel. He switched off the light and made himself comfortable to go to sleep; then, like a bolt from blue, a thought suddenly struck him: 'the postcard' – the one of Rio de Janeiro that Liam had presumably sent to his mother. Joe remembered that as well as having a picture of Christ the Redeemer on the front, it also had a picture of Copacabana Beach. Joe also remembered the date of the postmark that was on the postcard; it meant it would have been sent around the time Liam left the Premier Hill Suite Boutique Hotel. Maybe, just maybe, Liam sent his mother an obscure clue as to his whereabouts.

EIGHTEEN

JOE ARRIVED AT COPACABANA TWO DAYS LATER. He had stayed overnight in Sucre before travelling on to Copacabana. He got a coach from Asuncion to Sucre via Santa Cruz de la Sierra because it was the cheapest way to travel, but it had taken over seventeen hours to get there, then another sixteen hours from Sucre to Copacabana. He chose the cheapest hotel in Copacabana to stay in; it was called Hotel Utama and was just eight pounds a night for a single room, as Sally Devlin had told him that her funds were starting to dwindle. Due to this he made the decision to rent a bicycle rather than hire a car. He hoped there was a good chance that Liam had either stayed, or was staying, at the same hotel, but after enquiring with the hotel management they advised him that no one English fitting Liam's description had stayed there.

The town of Copacabana was even smaller than Nanawa; with just six thousand inhabitants, it was the main Bolivian town that was situated on the shore of Lake Titicaca. Joe had looked up images of the town while on the journey there, and while the beach beside Lake Titicaca was not as grand as the Copacabana Beach in Brazil, it was still very beautiful, and on the whole the town of Copacabana was extremely picturesque, way more so than Nanawa. Joe could understand why someone would prefer to live there over Nanawa, if indeed that was where Liam had moved on to.

Instead of starting with all pubs and restaurants like in Nanawa, he decided it would be best making enquiries at all the hotels and B&Bs first. Joe spent the majority of his first morning in Copacabana doing just that; however, nobody he spoke to said they had come across a young English man matching Liam's description from the photograph or the names Liam Devlin or Daniel Walker.

After some lunch Joe had made his way to the middle of the town centre. When he got there he saw a large monument; he walked over to it. It was a large sixteenth-century shrine titled the Basilica of Our Lady of Copacabana; he stood there admiring it when a street trader approached him trying to peddle his merchandise. The particular merchandise he was pushing were small porcelain statues of the shrine. Joe told him immediately he wasn't interested, but he was very persistent, like so many street pushers.

Joe removed the photograph of Liam Devlin from his trouser pocket and asked the trader if he recognised Liam, more as a diversion technique rather than genuinely believing that this guy might be able to help him. As he suspected the guy did not recognise Liam. Joe also mentioned the name Daniel Walker on the off chance that it would mean something to this guy. Of course it didn't, but this guy seemed genuinely interested as to why Joe was desperately trying to track down this man. Joe told him about who Liam was, when he went missing and why he believed Liam could be here in Copacabana.

The trader all of sudden started to get excited; he told Joe that this could be just a coincidence, but a couple of weeks ago a brilliant new player started playing for the local football club, C.F. Copacabana. This player, who is a striker, had helped the team to victory in their last three matches and had scored in all of them. The trader told him nobody knew much about this new player, but the rumour was that he was originally from England and signed as an overseas player for the club. Joe asked him what this player was called, his age and what he looked like. The trader told him he couldn't remember what the player's first name was, but his surname was Falconer, he was around six foot with long dark brown hair which he wore in a ponytail and has a beard. The man estimated the player's age to be early twenties. Joe asked the man for directions to the football club then bought one of his porcelain statues as he felt obliged to as he had been so helpful.

Joe started making his way towards the football club. The trader had informed him that the club was in one of the lowest leagues in Bolivia and most of the players were just semi-professionals. When Joe arrived at the stadium, if it could be called that, it had just one covered stand which looked more like an old shed and was the only part of the ground to have seating. The rest of the ground looked to be standing room only with a few safety barriers here and there. As he approached he noticed a small building to the right of the stadium that appeared to be the ticket office which doubled up as a souvenir shop. Joe had made the decision not to enquire about Liam, as if this English player was indeed Liam he didn't want word getting back to him from the club that an English private detective was trying to track him down just in case he fled the town. What he was going to do was enquire when the club's next home game was, and if it was not too far off he would buy a ticket so he could attend the game to get a good look at C.F. Copacabana's new English striker.

NINETEEN

JOE WAS STANDING ON THE TERRACE WAITING FOR the teams to emerge from the tunnel leading from the dressing rooms. He fortunately hadn't had to wait long for C.F. Copacabana's next home game as the member of staff he spoke to in the ticket office informed him they were playing just a couple of days later. Joe had brought his binoculars with him; before the match he had spent some time looking at YouTube videos of Liam playing for Leyton Orient, studying how he played, his running style and his mannerisms. According to the programme Joe had bought before entering the stadium, which was basically just four pages of black and white printed A4 paper, Billy Falconer's squad number was 9. However, when the teams came onto the pitch Joe couldn't see a player for the home side with the number 9 on the back of their shirt. It looked like Billy Falconer was not in the starting eleven.

Joe asked a supporter standing beside him if he knew why Billy Falconer was not playing; the supporter informed him Billy had picked up a slight knock in training the day before so as a precaution had only been named as a substitute for today's game. He pointed out Billy to Joe; the player he was pointing at was wearing a tracksuit top and was walking towards the home team dugout. Joe used his binoculars to get a good close look at Billy Falconer; his hair, as the trader described, was dark brown and tied back in a ponytail. He also had quite a substantial beard and his skin was quite tanned. Joe could not say for sure if this was Liam. If he had walked past him on the street when he first arrived Joe wouldn't have had the slightest suspicion it was Liam.

Joe played no real attention to the game; he spent most of the first half focusing on Billy Falconer to see if he could spot some tell-tale sign that it was actually Liam. He wished he had now paid the extra money for a seat in the grandstand, as it was on the same side of the pitch as the players' dugout. As it was nowhere near full he could have sat in a seat close to the dugout and may have been able to hear if this Billy Falconer spoke with a Cockney accent.

As the game went on it appeared more and more unlikely that Billy Falconer would play a part in this match; seventy-five minutes of the match had been played and C.F. Copacabana had already used two of their three substitutes. Two minutes later, though, C.F. Copacabana's opponents Padilla scored to go one-nil up. Joe hoped that this would be the catalyst for C.F. Copacabana to introduce Billy Falconer, but there was no movement coming from the home dugout. Four minutes later, though, Joe saw the C.F. Copacabana manager gesture towards the rest of the substitutes sitting on the bench in the dugout, then Billy Falconer stood up and removed his tracksuit top and started warming up on the side-line. A minute later the manager signalled to the referee, and when the ball next went out of play Billy Falconer came on to replace C.F. Copacabana's number 20.

It took a couple of minutes before Billy Falconer finally got on the ball, but no sooner had he received it and started running towards the opposition penalty area he got fouled and C.F. Copacabana were awarded a free kick which Falconer didn't take. It was another three minutes before Falconer got on the ball again; when he did Joe immediately recognised the running style as he dribbled his way past three players before unleashing a low right-footed shot that narrowly missed the left-hand post by a matter of inches. Billy Falconer only managed to get another couple of touches before the referee blew the final whistle, but from what little Joe had seen he was certain that this was Liam Devlin.

As soon as the match finished Joe quickly made his way out of the stadium and walked over towards the players' entrance; he would wait there until the players started to leave. He could see numerous cars in the players' car park; the vast majority were cheap bangers like Ladas and old Toyotas – football in Bolivia was a world away from the riches of the English Premier League.

Joe had left his bike chained to a lamppost outside the stadium. He assumed that Liam wouldn't have earned anywhere near enough yet to afford a car, even a cheap old banger, so unless he had got himself a moped or bicycle like Joe, he would probably be walking back to wherever he was residing.

Joe had to wait nearly twenty minutes before Liam came out into the players' car park. He didn't immediately start walking towards the exit; he stood in the car park for a few minutes conversing with some of the other players. Eventually the players started to disperse. Liam was walking with two other players towards the exit; Joe prepared himself to intercept Liam, but just a few short steps later they all turned left and got into an old blue Toyota Corolla. "Shit," Joe said to himself – Liam was getting a lift home. There was no way that Joe would be able to keep up with them on his bike.

He looked around; he could see there were a few taxis close by waiting to pick up what few spectators may still be hanging around the stadium or to pick up players who didn't have a car. Joe wheeled his bike over to the nearest one, but when he went over to the driver's window the driver told him he was waiting for someone. Joe didn't have time to try the other taxis as the car Liam was in was nearly at the bottom of the road. Joe waved four hundred boliviano, which was the equivalent of fifty pounds, at the taxi driver; this was more than enough to convince him to forget about his waiting fare and allow Joe to put his bike in the boot and get in. Joe asked him to follow the old blue Toyota Corolla ahead, which felt like a cheesy line that someone would say in a film. Joe didn't want to lose this chance to speak to Liam, as it would be another two weeks before C.F. Copacabana played again at home. Even though the players probably trained at the ground during the week, he didn't want to wait longer than necessary to speak to Liam if he could avoid it, as there was always the risk he might move on again.

They followed the car as it headed west; eventually it turned into a residential area then stopped outside an apartment complex. Joe ordered the taxi driver to stop about five hundred yards away – if this wasn't Liam's residence and they had to continue following the Toyota he didn't want to make it obvious. It wasn't Liam's residence, as the other passenger got out, waved, then headed towards the apartment. The car started to pull away, so they began to follow it again; it was heading back in the direction it had come from but continued east past the football stadium towards Lake Titicaca. It pulled up outside a small apartment block that was no more than one hundred yards from the lake's edge. Despite being in a lovely setting the apartment block wasn't looking in the best condition. Liam got out of the car, which drove off immediately, and started walking towards the apartment. Joe asked the taxi driver to pull over where the Toyota had been; he then quickly got out and shouted after Liam as he retrieved his bike from the boot.

"Liam!"

Liam spun round instantly. He stood there staring at Joe as he approached him.

"Liam, my name is Joe Wilde and I am—"

Joe didn't get time to finish his introduction as all of a sudden Liam turned and started sprinting. Joe jumped on his bike and started to give chase; he was glad he had brought it, as even though he was in reasonable shape there was no way he would be able to keep up with a nineteen-year-old professional footballer.

He was gaining on Liam at a rate of knots; he decided he wasn't going to jump off and tackle him to the ground, just explain who he was, and if Liam continued to run he would just follow him until he was out of breath. When he was almost on him, Liam suddenly darted right into a tight alley. At the speed Joe was riding there was no way he would make the turn; he slammed on his brakes hard and skidded past the entrance, then turned the bike around and headed down the alley. Liam was now a good forty yards ahead, but Joe was in no hurry as he knew he would catch up with him again easily. Liam, though, had started to throw various dustbins and flower pots that were up against the walls into the middle of the alley, so Joe had to slow his speed considerably in order to avoid the obstacles that were in his path. By the time he had manoeuvred past them all Liam had already exited the other end of the alley.

Joe didn't know if Liam had turned left or right. He started to peddle as fast as he could; he didn't want to lose sight of Liam completely. If he lost him now he would probably never find him again – nobody would. Joe was almost at the end of the alley when something large fell right across the exit. Joe immediately hit the brakes as hard as he could, but he couldn't prevent the inevitable, as his front wheel slammed right into it and he was catapulted through the air and landed on the ground twenty yards from his bike. Joe used his hands and arms to break his fall, but he still hit the ground hard. He turned his head to the right and saw Liam sprinting away. He wasn't as far away as Joe thought he would be;

he must have stopped to take a look at the result of his handywork.

Joe looked behind him. Liam must have pushed a large metal industrial bin on its side so it fell across the exit to the alley. Joe got up; his hands and arms were grazed slightly, but apart from that he was OK. He ran over to his bike, but when he looked down at it he could see the front wheel had completely buckled, so he would have to continue the rest of his pursuit on foot. He started running after him; Liam was now heading in the direction of the town centre, but they were quite some way from it. Joe suspected that Liam's plan was to make it to an area more populated, where it would be easier to blend in and lose him; however, at the rate Liam was extending his lead, he may lose sight of him well before he got there. Joe believed Liam had made a mistake, though, as he had chosen to run along the main road into the town centre, meaning there was a good chance taxis would be driving along it and Joe could possibly flag one down – unless, of course, Liam had the exact same idea.

It was as if Liam had read his mind, as he started waving at a taxi that was coming in the opposite direction. Joe prayed that it wouldn't stop – fortunately it didn't and just drove on past. As it did Joe could see Liam look over his shoulder then turn left onto another road; when Joe made it to the same road he saw that it went through an industrial estate. He looked up ahead for Liam, and as he did he saw him running across the road. A van pulled out onto the road at the same time, but Liam didn't notice it as he was paying far too much attention to Joe. The van driver honked his horn and slammed on the brakes while Liam spun around and quickly took evasive action by diving to his right. The van narrowly missed him by what must have been inches. The van driver shouted a few expletives towards Liam as he drove away. Liam had obviously hurt himself, as he was taking his time getting up.

Joe saw this as his opportunity, so he started to up his pace, although he knew he wouldn't be able to keep running for much longer. He got within twenty yards before Liam was up and running again, but he now had a limp and was clutching his leg so was not running at the pace he previously was. Joe caught up with him less than thirty seconds later; he reached out and grabbed the collar of Liam's tracksuit. Liam tried hard to keep moving and shrug him off, but he couldn't and gave up soon after. He turned round to face Joe. Joe tried to speak but was so badly out of breath he couldn't; he bent over, desperately trying to get some air into his lungs. He immediately regretted this because as soon as he did Liam punched him hard on the back of his head and took off again. The force of the blow nearly knocked Joe to the ground; it took him a few seconds to come to his senses. When he did he saw Liam go down the road where the van had pulled out.

Joe started to give chase again, but the sprint to catch up with Liam when he was lying on the road had really taken it out of him. He was probably running no faster than Liam was with his limp, and he knew he wouldn't be able to keep running for much longer. Joe had almost resigned himself to the fact he would lose Liam, but up ahead he noticed that Liam had suddenly stopped for some reason. He then realised why: the road they were on lead into a factory compound, but the compound gates were closed over and had barbed wire running along the top of it. Joe looked around; there were no side roads or alleys either, just high wire fencing along both sides of the road. Liam had run into a dead end.

TWENTY

Joe stopped around ten yards from Liam, who turned round to look at him.

"Don't kill me, please, I am begging you!"

"Liam, I am not going to kill you."

"I won't say anything to anyone, I swear."

"Liam, listen to me, I am not here to kill you. I—"

"You are one of them – you must be."

"One of who? Liam, please listen to me. My name is Joe Wilde. I am a private investigator and I was hired by your mother to investigate your disappearance. I managed to track you down – that is why I am here."

"No, you are definitely one of them. They are the only ones who could possibly track me down."

"Liam, who are they? I am not here to kill or even hurt you. I promise, you have to trust me, look." Joe turned out all his pockets and removed his jacket. "I am completely unarmed and if I really wanted to kill you,

I would have done it already. Look around – there is absolutely nobody here in close proximity. You have hurt yourself – let me take you somewhere you can receive medical attention."

"It's OK, I am not that badly hurt. I just twisted my ankle, that's all. Please, just go away and leave me alone."

"Liam, if that's what you want, fine, I will go, but please, just hear me out first. Like I said, I was hired by your mother to track you down. Your mother believed you were still alive – she refused to believe you would take your own life as you had so much to live for. If you are in trouble or danger I can help you – I have contacts."

"I don't trust you, and what's more, I don't believe you."

"Look, Liam, you don't have to believe me – call your mother and she will explain who I am."

"I-I can't."

"Of course you can."

"No, I can't," Liam said sternly. "As much as I would like to, I can't risk it."

"Why not? Liam, tell me what all this is about – why did you feel the need to fake your own suicide?"

Liam didn't reply; he just bent down and pulled his tracksuit trouser leg up to look at his ankle.

"You really need to get some ice on that. I will order a taxi to pick us up; we can go back to my hotel or back to your apartment – whichever you prefer."

"My apartment."

Joe used his phone to look online for a local taxi firm contact number, he asked Liam where their location was, then rang the number to make the booking.

"Taxi will be here in five minutes."

"My mum, how is she?"

"She is OK, considering."

"What about my dad, brother and sister – are they all OK?"

"I haven't met them, but I believe so. Obviously they are very concerned for your welfare."

Liam started to break down, so Joe decided not to push him for any more information.

They were back outside Liam's apartment ten minutes later. Joe paid the taxi driver then followed Liam towards the front door. Liam turned to face him.

"You wait out here. I am just going to get some ice then I will be back."

"Liam, I don't mean you any—"

"You wait here, I said!"

"OK, sure, whatever you want."

Joe watched Liam unlock his front door, enter his apartment then close the door behind him. Joe then heard him lock it again; he really was paranoid. Liam appeared a few minutes later holding an ice pack.

"I would prefer it if we talked in public, where there are witnesses. There is a bench over there just along the beach."

They walked over to the bench and sat down. They just sat there in silence for a minute while Liam held the ice pack against his ankle. Joe thought his best approach would be to wait for Liam to speak rather than try and force the issue.

Eventually Liam spoke. "So how did you track me down?"

"I discovered that you went into the internet café on Leyton High Road, to look up details on Nanawa. So I travelled to Nanawa, and when I was there I found out you worked at the Premier Hill Suite Boutique Hotel. I learnt from the manager that you had mentioned moving to Bolivia. How I managed to track you down to here in Copacabana was just pure guesswork."

"The postcard I sent my mum."

"That's right, the one with Copacabana Beach in Brazil on it. Why did you send it?"

"I don't know – was stupid, really. I suppose I just wanted to give her a glimmer of hope that I might still be out there. Something to cling on to so she didn't spend the rest of her life mourning the loss of her son."

"Why didn't you call your family?"

"I couldn't."

"But you did, though – call your mother at least."

"Yes, but I couldn't risk speaking. I just wanted to hear her voice again."

"Liam, who or what exactly are you afraid of? You have gone to extraordinary lengths. I mean, faking your own suicide then fleeing to another country – one where you don't even speak the language."

"I had no choice."

"Did you come up with this plan on your own or did someone suggest it to you and help you plan it?"

Liam didn't respond.

"Liam, I am going to phone your mother to tell her I found you. I really think you should speak to her as well."

Joe got out his phone and dialled Sally Devlin's number.

"Hello, Joe, any news?"

"Yes, Sally, and it's good news, I have found him."

"Oh my God, really? Where is he, in Copacabana?"

"Yes, he is here with me right now."

Joe could hear her starting to well up. "I don't believe it – oh, thank God, is he OK?"

"He is absolutely fine – well, apart from a slightly sprained ankle."

Sally Devlin was full on crying now. "Can I speak to him?"

"Sure."

Joe held out his phone and gestured for Liam to take it. He was hesitant at first but then slowly took it from Joe's hand. "Mum."

Joe thought it would be best to give him some privacy, so he got up and walked to the water's edge.

Joe had been walking up and down the beach for a good ten minutes before he looked over and realised Liam was no longer on the phone. He walked over to him; when he got there he could tell by the redness in his eyes that Liam had been crying.

"God, I miss them all so much. I wish I could go home, but I can't, not yet – maybe not ever."

"Did you tell your mother why you can't go home?"

"Not exactly – just told her that for my and the rest of the family's safety I couldn't."

"Liam, it is getting late and I am tired, especially after having to chase you on bike and then on foot through half of Copacabana."

This brought a slight smile from Liam.

"I am going to go back to my hotel – perhaps we can talk some more tomorrow? I am here to help you. Like

I say, I have contacts. I am sure you realise now that I mean you no harm. Are you free tomorrow morning? You don't have to go in for training or anything, do you?"

"No, I don't. I am free all day tomorrow."

"OK, well, I will call on you tomorrow morning at nine if that suits."

"Yes, OK."

"You are not going to flee the town, or the country even, I hope?"

"No, I won't, I promise. You have proven I can trust you."

"That's good. See you tomorrow, Liam."

TWENTY-ONE

JOE WOKE UP TO THE SOUND OF HIS PHONE ALARM
that he had set for 8am. He rubbed the sleep out
of his eyes; then got out of bed, which was more of a
struggle than normal as his muscles – in particular his
legs – were aching. The pursuit of Liam on bike and
then subsequently on foot had really taken a toll on his
body. It made him realise just how unfit he had become
since he left MI6. When he was in the shower he noticed
bruising that had been a result of his crash on the bicycle.

Joe had intended to walk to Liam's apartment, but due
to how stiff and sore he was feeling he got another taxi.
Joe had been successful in the first part of his mission –
finding Liam – now he had to find a way to persuade him
to come back to the UK.

Joe walked up to the front door and rang the bell;
he stood there for a minute, but there was no answer.
He rang again and waited, but there was still no answer.

Joe wondered if Liam had forgotten what time they had agreed and had popped down to the local shop or something, but he had this horrible nagging feeling that Liam had done another runner. He pushed the front door, not expecting it to be unlocked, but to his surprise it was. He peered inside and called out Liam's name; there was no answer. If Liam had scarpered then he had neglected to take his jacket with him, as it was lying on the back of a sofa in the living room, as well as the tracksuit top he was wearing yesterday evening, which was lying on the floor. It looked like Liam wasn't one for keeping things tidy, as the living room and kitchenette were a bit of a tip to say the least.

Joe decided to check upstairs; he called out Liam's name again, a little louder this time just in case he was still sleeping or in the bathroom – again, no reply. As he got nearer the top of the stairs he could see the bathroom straight ahead. The door was wide open; it was empty. To his right was Liam's bedroom. The door was partially open; as he approached he could see more clothes lying on the floor. He pushed the door open fully and to his horror he saw Liam lying on his bed on his back covered in blood. Joe rushed over and felt for a pulse; there was nothing and the body was stone cold.

Joe looked at Liam's lifeless body; there were multiple stab wounds to his torso and also one to his neck. The bed was literally soaked in blood. Joe just stood there in complete shock. He had witnessed death before many times when working for MI6, but this was different; it wasn't the shock of the dead body so much as the feeling of utter disbelief that after finally managing to track Liam down and discovering he was safe and well, less than twelve hours later he had been murdered.

He dreaded the thought of breaking the news to his mother. Joe looked around at the room: the majority of the contents in the drawers has been emptied onto the floor; there was a TV aerial cable hanging from a wall but no TV. Had Liam been the victim of a burglary gone wrong or had someone tried to make it look that way? Joe removed his phone from his pocket and called the police.

While Joe was waiting for the police to arrive he took a good look around the bedroom, being as careful as he could not to disturb the crime scene. There was a sliding door leading to a small veranda, but there was no sign of forced entry. He looked at the floor and then under the bed. There was no sign of the murder weapon, although with the state the bedroom was in it could be there under the heap of clothes and rubbish that was strewn all over the floor. Joe hoped the police might find it when they searched the room, but he didn't hold out much hope. He walked downstairs and had a good look round the living room; he hadn't noticed it when he first went in, but one of the windows was slightly ajar. He walked over to inspect it and saw that it had been forced open; this was how the intruder gained access to the apartment.

Joe walked outside and waited for the police; when they arrived he quickly briefed the scene of crime officers then waited outside for CID to show up so he could make an official statement.

TWENTY-TWO

IT WAS NEARLY MIDDAY BY THE TIME JOE RETURNED to the hotel; he went straight to the hotel bar. He needed a stiff drink, so he ordered a neat bourbon and took a seat far away from the few other customers who were there. He removed his phone from his pocket and set it on the table. He contemplated picking it up and contacting Sally Devlin, but he just didn't have the nerve right now; he just sat there staring at it.

Joe had spent half an hour in the bar sipping his bourbon; he really felt like staying in the bar for a few hours and getting drunk but decided against it as he still had to call Sally Devlin and wanted to be sober when he did. Perhaps he would raid the mini bar in his room afterwards, he thought to himself.

Joe knew he couldn't put off calling Sally Devlin any longer, otherwise she would learn of her son's death from the police first, which he didn't want. He decided he would make the call in his room. He got up, walked over to the elevator and pushed the call button. He really wished he could check out in the morning and fly back home, but the police advised him he would need to stay until they eliminated him from their enquiries. Joe got the impression that the Bolivian police didn't believe his explanation for being at the apartment or how he knew Liam. To be fair, though, if he was in their position and someone had told him that they were a PI hired to track down a professional footballer who faked his own suicide so he could move to a foreign country using various pseudonyms, then shortly after finding him he got murdered, Joe would probably find that too fantastical a story to believe as well. However, the police would be looking into Liam's background right now and they would find the various articles on Liam's 'suicide' online and he had given them Sally Devlin's contact number, so it shouldn't take too long for the police to clear him of suspicion.

When Joe entered his room he removed his phone from his pocket and flung his jacket onto the bed. He took a deep breath, hit the make call button then went to select Sally Devlin from his list of contacts. All of a sudden he heard a noise from behind him, but before he had time to turn around, he felt pressure on his throat.

Someone was trying to strangle him with a garrote wire. After the initial shock Joe had to think of something fast, otherwise his existence would be snuffed out within a matter of seconds. Joe was still holding his mobile phone, so his only option was to use it to hit his assailant in the head. Joe moved slightly to the left then repeatedly tried to hit his assailant over his left shoulder, aiming for their temple as best he could. After a few good strikes Joe could feel the garrote wire around his neck start to loosen. Joe continued to lash out despite the best efforts of his assailant to dodge his head out of the way, after landing one really good blow right on their temple the garrote wire loosened sufficiently for Joe to turn around just enough while putting his left hand between his neck and the garrote wire, then use his other hand to try and gouge his attacker's eyes out. The assailant, who Joe could now see was male, cried out then let go of the garrote wire; Joe flung it on the floor.

They squared off against each other. Joe was trained in Krav Maga combat, which he was taught by the UK Special Forces when he first joined MI6. The technique is essentially making multiple quick strikes to the weak points of the body such as the testicles, throat and eyes, then, after softening your opponent up, concentrating on the vitals like the ribs, kidneys and base of the skull.

Joe aimed quick blows to his opponent's throat and eyes, but his opponent was also clearly skilled in unarmed combat and evaded Joe's efforts easily while countering with blows to Joe's head and neck. Joe was able to withstand the impact well enough; fortunately his opponent was quite slight of build and Joe had come up against much bigger foes in his time, but what this guy lacked in power he made up for in speed.

They continued to trade blows while circling each other, but Joe was coming off worse – he was ring rusty, as it were. One nasty blow to the side of his head drew blood. All of a sudden the guy charged at Joe, which took him by surprise; he went in low and rammed his head hard into Joe's chest. The momentum from this pushed him hard against the far wall. Joe was slightly winded, but he responded by clamping his fists, raising his arms, then slamming them down hard like a mallet between his opponent's shoulders, which knocked him to the floor. When he was down Joe kicked him hard in the head.

The guy recovered from this better than Joe had anticipated and started to get back up, so Joe followed up with another kick to his stomach. The guy gasped and held his chest with one hand, but when Joe went to follow up with another kick his opponent blocked it with one arm then used his other arm to sweep Joe's standing leg from under him.

Joe went down hard on his back; as he did so he hit the bedside table with his shoulder. When he tried to bring himself back to his feet, his opponent, having grabbed the garrote wire off the floor, jumped on Joe's back, slamming him face down back to the floor. He straddled Joe and started to strangle him again. Joe tried desperately to shake the guy of his back, but to no avail. Joe felt his life slowly begin to ebb away. He believed this was it; this was how he was going to depart this world, but when he looked ahead he saw that the lamp that was on the bedside table had toppled onto the floor.

Joe stretched out his right arm and tried to grab it, he was just about able to touch it with his fingertips, but no more. With all the energy he had left in him Joe lurched forward as best he could – it was enough. He grabbed the lamp and smashed it hard against the side of the bedside table; the lampshade broke off. He then hit it a second time and the bulb smashed. With what felt like almost his last breath he flicked the switch that was on the base of the lamp, swung the lamp behind him and jabbed it into his attacker's thigh.

The guy instantly yelped and the garrote wire around Joe's neck slackened. Joe jabbed the lamp into him again and this time his opponent flopped onto the floor beside him. Joe ripped the garrote wire from his neck and struggled to his feet. When he got up he turned round to see his opponent trying to get back up. Joe picked up the lamp again, jabbed it into the guy's chest and held it there for a good ten seconds. The guy jerked and writhed on the floor as his muscles spasmed. Eventually he stopped moving and lay motionless.

TWENTY-THREE

JOE WONDERED IF HE HAD KILLED HIM; HE crouched over his body and felt for a pulse. He found one – the guy was unconscious. Joe looked at his face; he looked vaguely familiar, but Joe couldn't place it. He searched the guy's pockets for a wallet or any form of ID. There was nothing; however, there was a smartphone in his back trouser pocket. The phone was locked, though.

Joe picked up his phone, which now had a cracked screen, and called Mark, who would instruct him on how to unlock the guy's phone.

With Mark's help he was able to unlock the phone in less than a minute. When on the phone Joe had decided to leave out the details of how he had obtained this guy's phone as Mark would only have asked him numerous questions and he didn't want to spend any longer on the call than he had to just in case this guy either came to or had backup which could come bursting through his door any moment.

Joe looked through the phone; there were not many contacts on it and any text messages that had been sent to these contacts had been encrypted. It appeared that no inbound calls had been received and no outbound calls had been made from the phone. There were, however, some photos stored on it. At first they all appeared to be random pictures of people and places, but then Joe realised they were all pictures of him from when he was in Nanawa. He didn't realise this at first, as every picture of him – whether it was a fairly close-up shot or from further away – was with his back to the camera lens. They all seemed to be pictures of him walking away from the Gran Hotel del Paraguay. Joe looked again closely at the face of the guy lying sprawled out on the floor. "It couldn't be – surely not?" Joe thought to himself. His beard had been shaved off and his long hair was now slicked back, but the guy lying on the floor was the tramp he had spoken to briefly in Nanawa; Joe was almost certain.

Joe needed to get out now. He had obviously been under surveillance the whole time since he arrived in Paraguay, but who by? That didn't matter right now; he needed to leave the hotel without them realising. He couldn't risk checking out, as there could be more of them waiting inside the lobby. Joe thought it was best to change his clothes. In MI6 they had been taught counter-surveillance techniques. One of the techniques was to change your profile by altering your appearance. The problem was these people, whoever they were, had probably at some stage seen him wear all the clothes he had brought with him.

He changed anyway, into a T-shirt and a pair of trousers he hadn't worn for a few days. He then went into the bathroom, wet his hair and combed it into a neat side parting. He looked at himself in the mirror; he didn't look much different, but it was the best he could do. He left his jacket behind as he had worn it most days. He didn't bother packing; he just left the rest of his stuff in the room, apart from his wallet and flight ticket, which he put in his trouser pocket. He also took with him the guy's phone as Mark might be able to decrypt the messages for him, but he removed the battery from it, as they may well be able to track its GPS after this guy realises Joe must have taken it.

He left his room and took the stairs down to the bottom floor, but when he reached the bottom, instead of taking the door to the corridor that led to the lobby he walked in the opposite direction to the fire escape door instead. He pushed the release bar and walked out; he was in the car park at the rear of the hotel. They could well be covering the rear of the hotel as well, but Joe had no other choice.

He walked over to the wall on the far side of the car park; it was too high for him to jump up and grab the top, even when he tried standing on the bonnet of a car that was close to him. However, he spotted a large 4x4 a few spaces along that had been reverse parked against the wall. Joe walked over to it and climbed on the bonnet; he then clambered up onto the roof of the 4x4. As he did he saw out of the corner of his eye two men emerge from the side of the hotel and into the car park. As he climbed onto the wall he saw these two men scan the car park.

One of the men spotted Joe almost immediately. He turned to the other guy then pointed towards Joe; they then started sprinting in his direction. Joe quickly jumped down to the other side of the wall. He had dropped down amongst some trees and long grass, but when he looked ahead he could see a house close by – he was in someone's back garden. Right now trespassing on someone's property was the least of his worries. As he made his way through the trees and the long grass he came out onto a manicured lawn. He looked around; there was nobody in the back garden, but he could see movement inside the house. He heard the two men who were chasing him climbing the wall so he sprinted towards the side passage on the left side of the house. He ran through the side passage, which took him out onto the front driveway. There was a gate at the end of the passage which was open against the wall; Joe closed it behind him in order to slow his pursuers down to gain a few valuable seconds.

Joe ran out onto the street and headed left; a few seconds later he heard a car accelerating fast behind him. He looked behind him and saw a white 4x4 screech to a halt beside the driveway he had run out from; the two men who had been chasing him got in it. As Joe upped his pace the best he could he heard the screeching of tyres as the 4x4 accelerated after him. He knew they would gain on him in a matter of seconds, so he would have no choice but to run into someone's back garden.

Just as he had decided that was what he was going

to do he saw a couple walking hand in hand a few yards ahead on the other side of the road. He saw that they had come from an alley. Joe sprinted across the road and went down it. When he was roughly halfway down the alley he heard the 4x4 brake hard; he turned round, expecting to see at least one of the men get out and give chase, but it just sat there for a few seconds then sped off. Joe suspected they knew which street the end of this alleyway joined. Joe thought for a couple of seconds then made the decision to turn around and start running back the way he came.

Before he exited the alley Joe peered out just to make sure the coast was clear – it appeared to be. He stepped out and started running in the opposite direction to which the 4x4 had sped off in. He hadn't run more than twenty yards from the alley when one of the men jumped out in front of him from behind a large shrub. He was holding a gun and was pointing it straight at him. Joe heard footsteps coming from behind him; he glanced round and saw the other man approaching. It was a trap – they had lured him into a false sense of security. Joe heard the 4x4 approaching; it pulled up alongside him. The man behind Joe opened the nearside rear door while the other man gestured for him to get in. Joe walked slowly towards the door. He looked around and saw a few witnesses looking on, but this did not seem to concern his would-be kidnappers.

Just as Joe was about to get in, the man that was behind him told him to stop and put his arms out to the side; he came over and started to frisk him. First thing he felt was the phone Joe had taken from the guy that had attacked him in his hotel room. He removed it then continued to frisk him. Just then the noise of a siren could be heard in the distance, but it got louder and louder very quickly. A police car had turned on to the road and was fast approaching. Someone had called the police and there must have been a patrol close by considering how quickly it had appeared – luckily for Joe. The guy with the gun quickly lowered it and put it inside his jacket pocket. Joe saw this as his chance, he leant his head forward then jerked it back, as hard as he could, into the face of the guy who was standing behind him. Joe heard the sound of the guy's nose crack as he cried out. Joe spun round, pushed the guy to the side and quickly set off towards the alley again. The guy with the gun immediately gave chase while the other one, who now had blood streaming from his nose, got in the 4x4 as it sped off with the police car in pursuit.

TWENTY-FOUR

JOE RAN DOWN THE ALLEY; HE COULD HEAR THE footsteps of the guy behind him. Joe's plan was to try and make it to Liam's apartment, as he knew there would be police presence there. The problem was he didn't know exactly where he was in relation to Liam's apartment. He would need to try and put some distance between himself and his pursuer so he could get a look at the GPS map on his phone as this would slow him down when running. Right now he just needed to stay in reasonably populated areas so this guy would be reluctant to use his gun. When he was pointing the gun at him Joe got a good look at the guy; he was probably at least ten years younger than him and in better shape. Joe could sense him gaining on him.

Joe glanced back and saw the guy with his phone to his ear – he was probably calling for backup. He was only a few yards behind him now. Joe knew he would catch him any second, so he needed to do something to take this guy by surprise. Joe suddenly stopped in his tracks, spun round, moved slightly to his left and stuck out his right arm in line with the guy's throat. As the guy was so close to Joe he didn't have time to react and ran straight into Joe's rigid outstretched arm. He went down hard on his back. Joe kicked him in the head for good measure; he went to follow it up with another but the guy whipped out the gun from his inside jacket pocket. Joe aimed his kick at the guy's hand before he got a chance to aim the gun at him, and the gun flew out of his hand behind him.

Joe retrieved the gun and pointed it at him; he instructed him to get up slowly. As the guy was slowly getting to his feet Joe heard the sound of a roaring engine coming from behind him. He turned around and saw a motorcyclist heading straight for him at speed. Joe ran out to the middle of the road; the motorcyclist quickly changed direction to keep Joe in his sights. Joe headed for the nearest front garden, but with the speed the motorcyclist was travelling at he wasn't going to make it. When the motorcyclist was nearly on him, he dived to his right to evade it; the motorcyclist went straight on crashing into some shrubbery that lined the front of the garden. Joe heard the motorcyclist come off the bike.

The other guy was now moving towards him, but not very quickly; he was holding his back. Joe got up and started running down the road. He saw a car travelling towards him in the other direction; it wasn't driving fast or erratically, so he believed it wasn't part of the team that was after him. When the car was about one hundred yards away Joe stopped, held up the gun and aimed it at the car. The car started to slow down. Joe could see it was an elderly gentleman that was driving; he was the only occupant. When Joe was within roughly fifty yards the driver began to accelerate again and swerved to the other side of the road to avoid him. Joe had no choice but to move to the other side to try and block him as he once again heard the noise of the motorbike.

The driver slammed on the brakes and skidded to a halt just a few yards from Joe. Joe immediately ran to the driver's door, keeping the gun trained on the driver. He opened the door and grabbed the driver, who raised his hands and muttered, "Please don't shoot," in his native language. Joe shoved him out of the way, jumped in the car and hit the accelerator. He could see the motorcyclist just ahead; he would try and ram him off the road. He pressed the accelerator pedal right to the floor and veered to the other side of the road. The motorcyclist reacted just in time and swerved sharply to avoid him. Joe carried on travelling at speed; he saw in his rear-view mirror the motorcyclist do a quick U-turn and start to chase after him.

The car Joe had stolen was an old Nissan so wasn't equipped with a satnav. When Joe got to the bottom of the road he turned right; the motorcyclist was gaining fast. He looked up ahead and saw a set of traffic lights that were red. Joe had to hope that they would turn green by the time he reached them – fortunately they did. However, the traffic on this road was worse and Joe had to overtake several cars by going across into the opposite side of the road when it was safe to do so. The motorcyclist, of course, had no such problem and just drove straight down the middle in between the two sets of traffic. As a result he was on Joe's rear bumper in no time; this was not a problem as he couldn't try and ram Joe from behind or from the side on a motorcycle. What worried Joe was that the motorcyclist might have a helmet fitted with Bluetooth and call for support. Any moment now Joe was expecting to see 4x4s in his rear-view mirror as well as the motorcyclist.

Joe used his left hand to remove his phone from his trouser pocket; he wanted to bring up the GPS map so he could put in Liam's apartment as the destination, but as he was trying to do this there was a large bang and the rear window of the car smashed – the motorcyclist was now shooting at him. Joe chucked his mobile onto the passenger seat, picked up the gun and started blind firing over his shoulder. The motorcyclist swerved to his right and started accelerating; he was moving alongside the car. Joe couldn't go any faster due to the speed of the traffic ahead of him. He looked to his right and saw that the motorcyclist was almost level with his window and he was getting ready to aim and fire as soon as he had a good enough shot. Joe yanked the steering wheel hard to the right and rammed the side of the car into the motorbike; the motorcyclist lost his balance, flew off the bike and landed on the pavement. Due to the action Joe had taken, his car had mounted the curb and gone up onto the pavement; he saw a lamppost looming fast in his vision and yanked the steering wheel left, but it was too late – he crashed straight into the lamppost.

TWENTY-FIVE

For a minute Joe didn't know where he was. Somebody was touching him and also saying something; he then realised he must have got knocked out when the airbag deployed. He looked around for his phone – it wasn't on the passenger seat anymore. He then saw it on the passenger-side floor along with the gun. He picked them both up then tried to get out of the car, but a man – who he now realised was asking him if he was OK – would not get out of his way. He was telling Joe to stay put as an ambulance had been called and was on its way. Joe tried to explain that he was fine, but this guy would not listen.

Joe clambered over to the other side of the car and got out on the passenger side instead; he turned round to see a group of people huddled around the motorcyclist, who was trying to get up but struggling. Joe started to run away. He looked up the directions to Liam's apartment and was pleased to discover it was only five minutes away.

While he was making his way there he kept looking over his shoulder; every side street he crossed, every junction he came to, he was expecting motorcyclists and 4x4s to suddenly appear. On his way he passed a few shops; one of them was a tourist souvenir shop. In the shop window Joe could see they sold T-shirts and baseball caps. Joe went in and made his way to the back of the shop where the clothes were. There were T-shirts with a picture of Lake Titicaca printed on the front. Joe picked up one in his size and also picked up a C.F. Copacabana baseball cap. As he made his way to the till he noticed a sunglasses stand; he picked up a pair of the cheapest ones. After he paid for the stuff he walked to the back of the shop, bent down behind a rack of clothes and removed the shirt he was wearing, putting on the T-shirt. He then put on the baseball cap and sunglasses, bunched up his shirt, and threw it under the clothes rack. He walked out of the shop and continued to make his way to Liam's apartment; if they had seen him go into the souvenir shop they would have probably worked out pretty quickly that he had changed his appearance.

As Joe approached Liam's apartment he could see one police car parked outside. There was tape around the perimeter of the apartment and an armed officer was standing guard. Joe didn't want to get too close in case they recognised him; he walked over to the bench by the lake where he and Liam had sat the other night and called for a taxi to take him to the airport.

Joe kept the sunglasses and baseball cap on during the taxi ride to the airport – strictly speaking he shouldn't be leaving the country as he was under suspicion for murder. He would have some explaining to do when he arrived back in the UK, but he didn't have any choice. Whoever these people were who had killed Liam, they meant business; they were clearly efficient and well resourced. He would effectively be a dead man walking if he stayed in Bolivia.

TWENTY-SIX

ONE WEEK LATER

JOE WATCHED AS THEY LOWERED LIAM'S COFFIN into the ground; he looked across at Sally Devlin, who was struggling to hold back the tears. She was being comforted by her other son Brian, older brother of Liam, and her daughter Wendy, who stood either side of her amongst the rest of the Devlin relatives, including her ex-husband. It appeared Liam had come from a big extended family; the church service had been packed full, not just with family members but with many friends and colleagues of Liam. Joe assumed most of them were employed by Leyton Orient FC, but there were probably a good few from the wider football community as well.

The burial ceremony was to be for relatives only, but Sally Devlin had insisted that Joe attend. Despite being devastated by her son's death she was eternally grateful to Joe for managing to track Liam down, as if he hadn't she wouldn't have got to speak to him that one last time on the phone and tell him how much she loved and missed him. However, Joe couldn't shake the nagging feeling he had that if he hadn't managed to track Liam down, he might still be alive today.

When Joe had spoken with Sally a couple of days ago in his office he had explained to her that he had been in touch with the local police in Copacabana, but they had no leads regarding who murdered Liam. They were going with the theory that it had been a burglary gone wrong. He had explained to them why he had to leave the country so suddenly. They must have taken his explanation with more than a pinch of salt; he got the feeling the Copacabana police thought of him as some sort of Walter Mitty character. They had checked out his credentials and also spoke with Sally Devlin, and based on the evidence – or lack of it, as it were – they were happy to rule him out as a suspect. They did, however, make it clear that if new evidence came to light they may well need to contact him again. Joe had explained to Sally that even if there hadn't been an attempt on his life he still would have found the burglary-gone-wrong theory hard to swallow. He told her that the area where Liam was staying was not particularly affluent and the crime scene, apart from the blood, was too clean; there was a real lack of physical evidence, like fingerprints. Also according to the police report there were no foreign hairs or fibres found on Liam's body, not even under his fingernails; it appeared as if Liam didn't put up much of a fight – if any. Joe thought there was a possibility that Liam may have been drugged beforehand. The toxicology report had come back negative, but he suspected that the people who murdered Liam would have the resources to get hold of an untraceable substance.

With all the thoughts going round his head Joe found it very difficult to concentrate on what the vicar was saying after the coffin had been lowered. He only snapped out of his thoughts when the vicar asked the family members one at a time to pick up a handful of dirt and throw it on top of the coffin. The burial service finished shortly after this. Joe waited while the family members slowly started to disperse; he wanted to say goodbye to Sally and offer his condolences again.

After five minutes she walked up to him. "Thank you for coming, Joe."

"Not at all – it was the least I could do to come and pay my last respects."

Sally reached out and touched Joe's hand. "I wish you could have gotten to know Liam. He had his problems, but he was a lovely, good-natured boy."

"So do I. Given the turn-out it was obvious that he was very popular. It was a beautiful service and your eulogy was very touching, Mrs Devlin."

"Thank you, but please, call me Sally, we are friends now – well, I hope you feel that way and will stay in touch."

"Of course I will, Sally."

"And how are you, Joe?"

"Oh, I am OK."

"You could have easily lost your life as well."

"Well, it wouldn't be the first time I have faced death, although I thought those days were well behind me after I left MI6."

"Who do you think they were, Joe? And what do you think Liam was involved in?"

"I don't know who they worked for or who hired them, but my bet is they were paid assassins. As for what Liam was involved in, I have absolutely no idea, but if I can I will find out."

"I can't afford to pay you any more money, Joe."

"You don't have to, Sally. I am doing this for me as much as for you."

"Please take care of yourself, Joe."

"I will."

TWENTY-SEVEN

SIX WEEKS LATER

I T HAD BEEN A LONG EVENING; IT WAS APPROACHING 11:00pm and Joe was starting to get tired. He had started his surveillance at 6pm, but sitting and waiting in your car for five straight hours can make you tired. He had been hired by a big corporation to spy on one of their employees whom they suspected was passing on information to a rival company for money. The company had discovered work emails sent by this employee to a former employee of this rival company. There was nothing incriminating in the emails themselves, but this former employee was also the son of one of the directors. When her immediate supervisor questioned her over these emails she stated they met through a mutual friend and started to become friends, but after this the emails between the two suddenly stopped.

Joe had been working on this case for a week and a half; he had reported back to his current employer that this employee had recently bought a brand-new car – seemingly paid for up front, not on finance – and had also been on quite a few shopping sprees. His friend Mark had hacked into her private emails and bank accounts, but no large sums of money had recently been paid in and there had been no email exchanges between the two. Joe had seen this woman and the former employee of the rival company meet up once since he started his surveillance. It didn't look like his target was going to leave her apartment tonight. Joe decided he would wait until midnight and if there was no movement call it a night. Five minutes later, though, he saw the front door open and the woman walked out, locked the door behind her and got into her brand-new BMW 5 Series. Joe waited until she had pulled out of her driveway and had travelled a few hundred yards before starting his car to follow after her.

He had been following her for only a few minutes when she pulled into a petrol station and parked beside the nearest vacant petrol pump. Joe parked in a vacant car parking space that was furthest away from the shop entrance and watched her while she filled up her car. Joe was hoping that this was where she had agreed to meet her contact and where she would hand him an envelope with information, and in return he would hand her an envelope filled with cash.

He waited a few seconds after she had gone into the shop, then got out of his car and followed her in; he made sure he kept his distance the whole time and browsed to make it appear as if he was doing a bit of late-night shopping. However, in the short while she was in there no one approached her; all she did was pick up a litre of milk then go and pay for it, along with the petrol and a packet of cigarettes. She then walked out and got back in her car. Joe got back in his car and began following her again; however, all she did was drive back to her house and go back inside. Joe waited in his car for another fifteen minutes then decided to call it a day.

He started the journey back to his apartment reflecting on what had been another fruitless evening of surveillance. While on the journey Joe had noticed the car that was behind him had been so for the past five minutes. But not only that – he could have sworn that this car, which was either a dark blue or black Mercedes, had also been behind him when he drove from the petrol station back to his target's house. Was he being followed or was he just being paranoid? Ever since the events in Copacabana he had been in a heightened sense of paranoia, checking his mirrors regularly and constantly looking over his shoulder when out walking. He had toyed with the idea of getting a gun licence but instead carried with him a flick knife just in case.

***

"Morning, Jackie, you are in bright and early as usual."

"Morning, Joe, how did last night go?"

"Extremely uneventful, I am afraid."

"Sure, at least it's regular income."

"True, has anything new come in?"

"Yes, a man rang and asked to speak with you."

"Right, did you take his number?"

"No, he wouldn't give it to me – it was all a bit strange, to be honest."

"How do you mean, strange?"

"Well, first off he wouldn't give me his name. He said he wanted to speak to you in person, so I suggested he call in, but he insisted you meet him at a place of his suggestion."

"Did he even say what he wanted to see me about?"

"Yes, he did. He said it was about Liam Devlin; he said he knows who killed him."

"But he didn't give you a name?"

"No, he just said he would make contact with you. What do you think, Joe – a crank call?"

"I would say more than likely, Jackie. The fact he wouldn't give his name or leave a phone number for me to contact him makes me more than just a little suspicious. Was there anything else?"

"No, that was it. Don't forget that you agreed to meet Phil for lunch today."

"Oh, yes, thanks for reminding me."

Joe spent the majority of the morning going through his emails and correspondence; he also spoke briefly to the CEO of the company called Headstart Technologies that he was currently working for. There wasn't enough work for him to fill up the whole morning; by 11:30 he was willing 12pm to come around more quickly so he could enjoy a long lunch with his mate.

They had agreed on meeting at the bistro round the

corner from Joe's office like they so often did – more out of habit and convenience rather than because the food was anything special. Joe walked in and looked around, but Phil was not there yet. He sat down at a table and browsed the menu while he was waiting. After he had decided on what he was going to order his phone buzzed; it was a text message from Phil saying he was running late. He would be another ten minutes, so he asked Joe to go ahead and order the mushroom risotto for him. Just after Joe sent a text in reply a man came up from behind him and set down a newspaper on his table.

"I am finished with that, mate, if you want it."

Joe looked up from his phone to say thanks, but the guy was already walking towards the door. He looked down at the newspaper. It was a copy of *The Times*. He immediately noticed something had been written in pen in the top right-hand corner; it said, "I am serious about what I told your secretary – meet me in Manor Park beside the fountain at 5:30pm tomorrow evening. You must come alone, otherwise I will not show up."

The waiter came over and Joe ordered for himself and Phil. Five minutes later Phil arrived.

"Hi, buddy, sorry I am late."

"No worries, mate, I have ordered for us – should be here shortly."

"Cheers. So how is your current case going? Any closer to getting the evidence the company require?"

"No, but it is still quite early days."

"Do you think this woman is actually selling company secrets?"

"I don't know, but all the money she has recently

been splurging has to come from somewhere. Anyway, how are things over at Thames House?"

"Oh, you know, just the usual."

"No more potential terror plots from the National League?"

"There is no intel to suggest they are planning something else, but as you know we can never be one hundred per cent sure."

"What about the attack on the mosque? No closer to making any arrests? You were able to apprehend and arrest their leader very shortly after their previous attack which killed Malcolm Walcott."

"No, unfortunately not – there isn't enough conclusive proof to point to a particular member or members of the National League."

"And they are still denying responsibility for the attack – is there a possibility it wasn't actually them?"

"No, it was them alright."

The waiter brought their food to the table and they tucked in. Joe picked up *The Times* newspaper that he had put on the seat beside him and put it on the table. "Jackie took a call this morning from a guy who said he knows who killed Liam. He didn't leave a name or a number for me to contact him back."

"Just a hoax caller, then."

"Probably, but while I was waiting for you a man came up to me and dropped this newspaper on the table. He said I could have it as he was finished with it then walked out. But he wrote something on the front before he gave it to me." Joe turned the paper round so Phil could read what had been written on it.

"So what did this guy look like?"

"I didn't get a good look at him. He walked up from behind me, threw the paper down then when I looked up he was already walking towards the door. I didn't get a look at his face. Also he was wearing a hat."

"I see. You didn't get a sense of what age he was – his ethnicity, height, anything like that?"

"He was Caucasian, average height, probably middle-aged, but, like I said, I didn't get a look at his face and it all happened in a matter of seconds."

"So are you going to go to the park tomorrow evening just on the off chance that this guy may be on the level? I mean, even if he isn't, what have you got to lose?"

"Er, my life – have you forgotten what I told you happened to me in Bolivia? It could be a set-up. I could be walking into an ambush."

"Sure, the park is a very public place. It's not like he has asked you to meet him late at night. There will be plenty of people about."

"Even so."

"Look, why don't I come with you? For backup."

"He is insisting I turn up alone. He states that if I bring anyone with me he won't show up."

"I mean, incognito – I could go there early to scan the area, then if everything looks OK I will text you to let you know. If this guy shows I could observe out of sight and if anything remotely dodgy or suspicious happens I will alert you."

"I suppose."

"Come on, Joe, you never know. This guy may have

all the answers to the whole Liam Devlin affair. If you don't go and he never contacts you again you could spend the rest of your life wondering what if."

Joe knew Phil was right; as unlikely as it was that this guy knew anything or that he would even show, he owed it to Sally and Liam to at least go on the off chance.

TWENTY-EIGHT

JOE WAS IN HIS CAR; HE WAS PARKED A COUPLE OF miles away from Manor Park. He looked at his watch – it was 5:15. Phil said he would text him at twenty-five past; he had gone to the park at 5pm to walk around and scan the area around the fountain. Joe removed a cigarette from the packet and lit it. He hadn't smoked for years, but he needed something to calm his nerves. After he had returned from Copacabana his anxiety levels had been off the scale; he had gone to his local GP, who prescribed him a course of Valium. As the weeks passed his anxiety levels returned to normal, but ever since he decided to meet with this guy he could feel the anxiety rising again. At 5:25 on the dot he received a text from Phil saying, "All clear here, you are good to go." Joe turned on the engine and started to make his way to the park.

It took Joe three minutes to arrive at the park, then another minute to make it from the main entrance to

131

the fountain. Joe stood by the fountain then had a look around; there were quite a few people milling about. But nobody seemed to be taking any particular interest in him. He stood and waited.

Joe had been waiting for five minutes and there was no sign of anyone coming to approach him; there was a bench close by that a couple of people had been sitting on, but it was now vacant. He went over and sat on it.

Another five minutes had gone by and there was still no sign of this guy. Joe decided he would give it another five minutes. His phone buzzed; it was a text from Phil. "Looks like you were right, mate – obviously just a crank. Shall we leave?" Joe was in the process of texting back when he suddenly felt the presence of someone sit down at the other end of the bench. Joe turned his head to look.

"Don't look at me, Mr Wilde, just stare straight ahead or at your phone. We might be being watched."

"Who by?"

The man didn't answer. "Obviously you know, Mr Wilde, that Liam faked his suicide. Well, I helped him do it – I also helped him flee the country."

"Who are you?"

"Who I am is not important right now. What I am about to tell you is."

"And what is that?"

"Before I tell you, Mr Wilde, I need to make something very clear. You cannot pass on this information to anybody else – not even Sally Devlin – because if you do you are putting your life in danger as well as Sally's, or anyone else you tell for that matter.

Nobody must ever find out the information I am about to tell you or where you got the information from – do you understand?"

"When you say my life is in danger, can I assume you are referring to the people who tried to kill me in Copacabana?"

"Yes."

"Who are they?"

"They were hired assassins."

"I had worked that much out already. Who hired them?"

"They were working for MI5."

"What? That's preposterous."

"Look, Mr Wilde, a lot of what I am going to tell you will be hard to believe, but it is no less than the truth."

"Who the hell are you and why on earth should I believe you?"

"I myself am an MI5 agent."

"OK, so what is your name and what branch do you work for?"

"Were you not listening to what I said to you at the start, Mr Wilde? Who I am is not important. You don't need to know that. I am already putting myself at risk just speaking to you now; I am not going to take any more undue risks by giving you my name. If you were to let this information slip I can't have this being linked back to me."

"Do you know what I think, Mr whoever you are? I think you are just a fantasist and you are just playing out one of your fantasies right now by pretending to be an MI5 agent."

"Then how would I know about the people who tried to kill you in Copacabana? I know you told the local police about it, but the police never released that information to the press. And just in case you were in any doubt, they were the same people who killed Liam."

"OK, let's just pretend for one minute I believe you – why on earth would MI5 want Liam Devlin killed?"

"To keep him quiet – he knew too much."

"Knew too much about what exactly?"

Just then there was a loud bang – it sounded like a gunshot – which startled Joe and this man.

The man got to his feet and started running; as he ran he shouted back to Joe, "Fuck, this could be them. If I were you, Mr Wilde, I would start running for your life."

"Wait," Joe shouted after him, but he was already halfway towards the main gate.

Joe started running as well, but Phil suddenly came running towards him.

"Hey, did you hear that, Phil?"

"I did – at first I thought it was a gunshot, like you and this man clearly did, but I think it was just a car backfiring. I certainly haven't seen anyone with a gun."

They both looked around to scan the surrounding area. Nobody else looked remotely concerned, but then Joe knew most ordinary people wouldn't automatically assume the worst; they would put it down to a backfiring car or something else. Those who are in or were in the secret services like himself and Phil were hardwired slightly differently; they were trained to assume anything and everything might be a threat.

"I think you are right, Phil – probably just a backfiring car."

"Yeah, I think so. Anyway, it certainly put the frighteners up your friend – he certainly didn't hang about, did he?

"No, he certainly didn't."

"So what did he have to say? Did he tell you who killed Liam?"

"He did, yes."

"And?"

"He said MI5 hired people to do it."

"Really? Well, I must say, that is an interesting theory. And did he also tell you who was the second gunman on the grassy knoll in the Kennedy assassination while he was at it?"

"Yeah, I know it's ridiculous. The thing is, though, he said he himself is an MI5 agent."

"Yeah, and I am the fairy godmother."

"The thing is, he said he knew about the attempt on my life in Copacabana. That wasn't public knowledge – how could he have possibly known that?"

"That is interesting, but here, you are not going to take this guy seriously, are you? He is clearly a delusional nutjob."

"But if he is an MI5 agent, that would possibly explain how he knew about the attempt on my life."

"Well, I can check this guy out for you if you like. What did he say his name was?"

"He didn't."

"Or tell you the branch of MI5 he works in?"

"No, he said he would be putting himself at too much of a risk if he did."

"Well, that's convenient. Look, mate, this guy was obviously just having you on. How he knew about the attempt on your life in Copacabana, who knows – just because something isn't public knowledge doesn't mean it can't get leaked. Maybe he was over in Copacabana or knew of someone who was and witnessed those people chasing after you there. Copacabana in Bolivia does attract the tourists, I believe – or it could just have been a lucky guess."

"Yeah, you are probably right."

"Anyway, if he is genuine I am sure he will try to contact you again to tell you the rest of what he knows."

TWENTY-NINE

JOE WAS SITTING BEHIND HIS DESK SIPPING HIS cup of tea; just a few minutes ago he had finished an hour-long meeting with a client. Two weeks had passed since his meeting with the man who claimed to be an MI5 agent in Manor Park and he had not been back in contact. He decided to go on the internet and catch up on the news while on his tea break. The mosque bombing was still dominating most of the news headlines. One of the headlines caught Joe's attention; it asked the question of whether the Hackney Central Mosque bombing was a conspiracy. It was from an obscure independent news site.

Joe clicked the link to bring up the article; it gave details of accounts from a few eyewitnesses who claimed the bombing wasn't real and there were not as many casualties as reported by the media. Some even claimed there were no casualties at all. There were links to view mobile phone video footage from several of the witnesses, who stated their footage proved their claims; the victims appeared to be dummies as there were no missing limbs. Joe couldn't believe what he was reading; he had been there, witnessed the aftermath. The victims he attended at the scene were real people and he had got covered in their blood, yet here were people claiming that the bombing wasn't real. It made Joe's blood boil. Why was it that after nearly every terror attack there were always certain people in society that couldn't accept the truth and offered up crazy conspiracy theories instead? What made it even worse were certain news sites like this one giving these lunatics a platform to push their ridiculous theories. It was an insult to the people who had lost their lives.

There was a knock on his office door; Jackie poked her head round. "Joe, Liam's father William Devlin has come in; he would like to speak with you. Is it OK to send him on in?"

"Yes, that is fine, send him on in."

Joe had only spoken with William Devlin a couple of times before; he was almost ten years older than Sally and had thinning hair which was shaved very short. He worked as a long-distance lorry driver.

William Devlin walked into the office. "Hello again, Mr Wilde, thanks for agreeing to see me."

"Not at all, Mr Devlin. Please, take a seat."

"Thank you."

"Would you like a cup of tea or coffee?"

"No, that's OK, I am fine, thanks. As you know, Mr Wilde, Sally and I have quite a strained relationship. We tolerate each other for the sake of the kids – well, to be more accurate, she tolerates me."

"To be honest, Mr Devlin, Sally really didn't mention you much or how exactly things are between you."

"Well, we don't really talk. I think if Sally could have it her way I wouldn't be in her or the kids' lives at all. The point is, Mr Wilde, that she never really told me much about your investigation. The majority of what I know I read in the papers. I overheard my son and daughter discussing what happened to Liam in Copacabana, that it is very unlikely he was the victim of a burglary gone wrong despite what the police said, especially given what happened to you. What happened over in Copacabana, Mr Wilde? Please, I would like to know."

"The day Liam's body was discovered there was an attempt on my life. I was very lucky to get back here alive."

"Bloody hell, do you believe that Liam's murder and the attempt on your life are connected?"

"Yes, I do."

"Why would someone want to kill my son and you? And why did he fake his own suicide so he could run away in the first place?"

"Believe me, Mr Devlin, I would love to know that just as much as you and Sally. As an educated guess I would say that Liam either witnessed something or found out about something illegal and was killed as a result. Those same people must have assumed Liam told me what he knew and that's why they tried to kill me."

"So Liam never told you why he fled the country?"

"No, he was scared and extremely paranoid when I found him. He thought I had come to kill him. Even when he realised that was not the reason I had tracked him down, he didn't fully trust me. I was slowly beginning to win his trust and I believe he would have told me had he not been murdered."

"Sally said that you were going to investigate his murder free of charge."

"Yes, to a certain extent. Obviously I can't work on the case full time as I need to earn a living, but if there are any new leads I will follow them up."

"Have you got any new leads right now?"

"Not really, no. Look, Mr Devlin, is there anything in Liam's past you can think of – anything at all, no matter how unlikely or insignificant – that could possibly be linked to what happened to him?"

"No, not that I can think of. Liam had a very normal and very happy childhood – ask anyone."

"How did he deal with the breakup of your marriage to Sally?"

"Well, obviously he was a little upset, as you would expect, but he got over it quick enough. His football career was always his main focus. Also he was sixteen, not far off an adult. Perhaps if he had been younger when Sally and I separated it might have hit him harder."

"Why did you and Sally break up, Mr Devlin, if you don't mind me asking?"

"It was just one of those things – no particular reason. We just grew apart, I suppose."

"You said earlier you believed that if it was up to Sally she would prefer not to have you in her and your kids' lives. To me that would suggest it was more than just a case of two people growing apart."

"OK, Mr Wilde, I will be honest with you, I have done a few things in my past that I am not proud of and regret, such as being involved in brawls in pubs and behaving inappropriately."

"Behaving inappropriately?"

"I suppose you could call it being racist – certainly using racist language from time to time. About four years ago I was made unemployed and for a year I couldn't get another job for love nor money. I spent most of the time spending what little money I had down the pub or in the bookies. I was mad at the world and I felt like a failure. One day when I was in the bookies I got speaking to another punter who was in the same position as me; he said the main reason why it was so hard to find jobs was due to the amount of immigrants, particularly ethnic minority immigrants, as they are willing to do the same jobs as us Brits but for less pay. And some employers are employing ethnic minority workers even though they may be less skilled or have less experience just to meet diversity quotas or to promote diversity. At the time it all seemed to make sense; he also told me about his younger sister who had been the victim of sexual abuse at the hands of a group of Muslim paedophiles. He said he was a member of the National League and that the guy who owned the bookies was one of the founding members. He told me to follow him to an office in the back of the bookies where he introduced me to the owner. His name was Frank Parker."

"Frank Parker was one of the founding members of the National League?"

"You know him?"

"Yes, early on in my investigation into Liam's disappearance I questioned him, as I found out that Liam owed him fifteen grand."

"I knew that Liam's owed money to some bookies, but I didn't know that Frank was one of them."

"Before going to meet Frank Parker I had a good look into his background. I found nothing about him being one of the founding members of the National League."

"No, you wouldn't. He is effectively just a silent member; he is the main donator to the organisation. He told me that he doesn't want to be publicly linked to the group because the publicity would be bad for his businesses. He told me why he and two other guys decided to form the National League and what its purpose was. He told me I should go along to their next rally, so I did. There were hundreds of people there and listening to the main speaker really struck a chord. I signed up as a member soon after that. After joining I felt like my life had purpose again and I made new friends."

"So I take it Sally wasn't exactly over the moon when you told her you had joined the National League?"

"Yes, you could say that. I suppose that was the beginning of the end for us, but what really upset her was when I tried to involve Liam."

"In what way did you try to involve him?"

"Well, when he was fifteen I used to take him down the pub with me when I was going to meet up with other members of the National League. At first it was just for the banter, but after a while we started to explain our ideology to him and the purpose of the National League. He then started to come along with me to some of the rallies and meetings. My aim was to get him interested enough and to believe in our cause so that when he turned eighteen he would be interested in signing up as a member. The fact that Liam was a rising football star who would likely go on to play for England would give the National League more exposure in the media. However, when Liam told his mum what I had planned for him she hit the roof. She told me that being married to a racist and fascist was bad enough, but there was no way she would ever allow Liam or any of our children to go down the same path. She threw me out of the house there and then and told me she would be going to her solicitor about divorce proceedings."

"Are you still a member of the National League?"

"No, I left after only a year and a half. I don't even socialise with any of the members – Sally would never allow me to see the kids if I was. That is not the only reason why I left, though. When I joined the National League they were not a violent organisation. Yes, some of the members may have got involved in fights and sometimes got arrested for inciting racial hatred, but it was mostly just marches, rallies and peaceful protests – nothing like what it has become now. When the National League started to turn to terrorism, I knew it was wrong, and then I started to see the majority of the members –

especially the higher-ranked ones – for what they really were. You have to believe me, Mr Wilde, when I say I truly regret ever being a part of that organisation and for trying to indoctrinate Liam."

"Did Liam show any interest in the National League after you and Sally split up? Or perhaps started to get interested in them again more recently?"

"No, definitely not, Mr Wilde. He was only ever interested in playing football and being the best he could possibly be. Just like me he was disgusted when the National League started carrying out acts of terrorism. Leyton Orient has quite a few foreign players and a couple from ethnic minority backgrounds – Liam got on very well with all of them."

"OK, well, like I said, if I uncover any new leads I will chase them up and I will keep you informed, Mr Devlin."

"Do you think there is a possibility the National League could have been responsible for Liam's murder?"

"I think it is unlikely, but I certainly wouldn't rule it out."

"Why would the National League want to kill Liam?"

"I don't know, but like I said, I think that it is unlikely. There could be some connection between Liam's death and the National League, even if they aren't responsible for his death."

"So I have given you a possible lead then?"

"Of sorts – I will certainly make some enquiries."

"Thank you, Mr Wilde."

"Not a problem. I will be in touch, Mr Devlin."

THIRTY

JOE SAT IN THE CAR PARK OF NORTH WALTHAMSTOW Forest College. He had travelled from John Wilcox's home, where he had called, but there had been no answer. Joe assumed John must have a lecture that morning. When he got there he saw John's car in the car park. It was 11:30; Joe decided he would wait until noon to see if John came out to go for lunch or back home if he was finished for the day – if not he would go into the college canteen to try and find him.

Joe had sat in his car waiting; when it got to 12:15 he decided he had waited long enough, so he got out and made his way to the front entrance. Once inside he followed the signs for the canteen. When he reached it he couldn't believe the amount of students that were in there; it was going to be like searching for a needle in a haystack. Joe now wished he had asked John for his mobile number the last time they met. He started asking various students if they knew John Wilcox and if they had seen him in the canteen. After five minutes of asking around he got speaking with a group of students that were on the same course as John and they pointed out to Joe the table John was sitting at. As Joe walked over he could see John sitting with two other male students.

"Hello again, John."

"Oh, it's you – what do you want?"

"Charming, John. Do you mind if I speak with you for a few minutes?"

"Why? As you managed to find Liam you must know now that I had nothing to do with his disappearance, so there should be no reason you need to speak with me, or are you going to accuse me of flying over to Bolivia to kill him now?"

"Look, John, I was just doing the job I was hired to do, and if you had been completely honest with me from the start I could have ruled you out as a suspect a lot earlier."

"So what is it you want to speak with me about?"

"I would like to know if Liam ever mentioned the National League to you?"

John looked at his two mates then looked at Joe again. "Give me ten minutes to finish my lunch and I will meet you out in the car park."

"OK, I will wait in the car park for you."

Joe didn't even have to wait ten minutes before John Wilcox walked out into the car park. He walked over to Joe, who was leaning against his car.

"The answer to your question is yes, Liam did mention the National League to me."

"What did he tell you?"

"We were talking about his mother and father and I asked Liam how he thought they would react if he ever told them he was gay. He then told me about how his father used to be a member of the National League and that he sometimes took Liam with him to the rallies and he often went with his father to the pub for drinking sessions with fellow members."

"Did he ever mention anyone in particular from the National League or a specific incident during this period when he was hanging around with some of the members?"

"No, he didn't – well, apart from…"

"Apart from what?"

"Well, one day we were talking about former lovers and also the circumstances regarding each other's first-ever homosexual encounter. Liam told me his first was with a guy who was a member of the National League when he was sixteen."

"Really? Did he tell you the name of this member?"

"No, he said he couldn't just in case word got out. Even though the National League is primarily against uncontrolled immigration and Islamic extremism, I believe homophobia is quite rife in the organisation, as you might expect. I mean, being gay isn't seen as being particularly macho."

"Did he say anything about this guy at all? For example his age, what he looked like? Anything like that?"

"No, all he said was he was a great lover. In fact, he mentioned that a few times – it made me feel a little bit insecure."

"Now, are you sure you have told me everything you know about this guy?"

"Yes, honestly – I wouldn't keep anything from you. I have already learnt that lying to you is pointless as you always seem to find out the truth in the end."

Joe thanked John for his time and walked back to his car; this time he had got John to give him his mobile number just in case he needed to contact him again. He sat there thinking about what John had just told him. Was it possible that Liam did become part of the National League after all, but perhaps just as a silent member, like Frank Parker? Could he have been involved in some of their terror attacks in recent years? Maybe that would explain why MI5 were after him; then again, if they were after him, why kill him? Surely arresting and then interrogating him would have been enough. That's if MI5 were even after him in the first place. He really felt like he wasn't getting any closer to finding out the truth.

Joe suddenly realised that John Wilcox hadn't gone back inside; he was still standing in the car park. He looked back towards Joe then looked away again. He then saw him check his watch; a few seconds later he glanced over in Joe's direction again. About a minute later Joe saw him begin to slowly walk towards the front entrance. Joe turned on the engine and slowly started driving towards the exit; as he was approaching it he kept checking his rear-view mirror. Just before he exited the car park he saw John turn around with his phone to his ear and start walking towards the car park again. Joe needed to find out why John Wilcox was acting so suspiciously.

He turned into the first side road that he came to and parked his car. He retrieved his binoculars from the glove compartment and walked quickly back towards the college car park. Joe didn't go back into the car park; he just stood on the other side of the road opposite a gap in the trees that lined the car park. Through the gap he could see John Wilcox standing on his own at the back of the car park. A minute later a car drove into the car park; John Wilcox started to walk towards this car after it had parked up. The driver got out and they both walked over to John's car and got in.

Joe zoomed in on the driver-side window as best he could, but the reflections of the trees on the car window meant his view was far from ideal. It looked like they were just talking, but then Joe saw John hand the guy something; this guy started shuffling whatever it was and Joe realised he was counting cash. He put the money in his pocket, then Joe saw him hand John a package of some sort. A few seconds later the guy got out of the car and walked back towards his own. Joe kept his focus on John; as best he could tell it appeared John had taken something out of the package and put it in his coat pocket then put the package in his glove compartment. John got out of his car and went and stood at the back of the car park. Joe saw him take out his phone; it looked to Joe as if John was texting.

A couple of minutes later Joe saw a girl – presumably another student – walk up to John. They exchanged a few words then this girl handed John some money. Joe saw John put the money in his trouser pocket then remove whatever he had put in his coat pocket earlier and hand it to the girl, who subsequently put it in her handbag as she walked off. Joe had witnessed enough drug deals in his time to realise this was what had just taken place.

The man that had given John the package of what must have been drugs hadn't yet driven off. Joe focused the binoculars on his driver-side window and saw the guy talking on his phone. Low-level drug-dealing such as this didn't concern Joe – he wasn't a cop – but he believed it was his civic duty to try and track down a major drug pusher if he had the opportunity. Joe started running back towards his car; he was going to wait for this guy to exit the car park then follow him.

THIRTY-ONE

JOE FOLLOWED THE CAR INTO HACKNEY TOWN centre. The guy parked his car on the same street where Frank Parker's bookies was located. Joe had parked a couple of hundred yards down on the opposite side of the road. Joe, with his binoculars, again looked closely at this guy; he was on his phone again.

Ten minutes had gone by and this guy was still sitting in his car. He was no longer on his phone; he was smoking a joint. Joe had to wait another ten minutes before something interesting happened. Two men walked up to the car and stood beside the driver door. Joe saw the guy lower his window and hand to each of the two men a sum of cash. These guys then turned around and started walking in the direction Joe was parked. Joe watched them closely as they walked up parallel to his car, then turned his head to keep an eye on them as they walked on past. Joe then saw these two men go inside the bookies. Joe got out his phone and called John Wilcox; there was no answer, so Joe left him a voicemail stating there was something else he had meant to ask him and requested he call him back.

It was after 10pm when John Wilcox eventually called Joe back, who was sitting in his living room watching the news. Joe turned down the TV volume and answered the call.

"Hi, John, thanks for calling me back."

"No problem – what is it that you forgot to ask me?"

"Well, actually there wasn't anything else at the time, but there is something now, that's why I needed you to call me back."

"What is it?"

"Listen to me, John. I am not going to turn you into the police, so you don't need to worry about that, just so long as you tell me who supplies the drugs that you sell."

"Joe, I don't know what you are talking about."

"Look, John, spare me the act – even you said yourself that I always find out the truth in the end. I witnessed you and another man get into your car, then saw you hand this guy some money before he handed you a package. Then after the guy got out of your car I saw you remove something from the package and put it in your coat pocket. You then sold the weed, cocaine, ecstasy – whatever it was – to a female student who came out and met you in the car park."

"So you were spying on me?"

"I wouldn't have felt the need to spy on you if you hadn't acted so suspiciously in the car park. Like I said, I won't involve the police, John, so long as you give me the name of the person, or people, who supply you the drugs."

"Why do you need to know their names?"

"So I can pass this information on to the police. Don't worry, I will leave your name out of it. Your parents seem fairly wealthy, so I don't know why you felt the need to get involved in drug-dealing."

"I didn't have any choice. I have to."

"What do you mean, you don't have a choice? Who was that man who supplied you with the drugs this afternoon?"

"All I know is he is called Paul. I don't know his surname – he never gave it and I never asked."

"How did you meet him?"

"Through someone else."

"That someone wouldn't be Frank Parker, would it?"

John didn't answer immediately, but the silence from the other end pretty much confirmed to Joe it was. "What makes you think that?"

"Because I tailed the guy who supplied you with the drugs. He parked a few hundred yards away from Frank Parker's bookies. I then saw him hand a load of rolled-up notes to two guys who walked up to his car window; these two guys then went into the bookies straight afterwards. Why are you selling drugs for Frank Parker? You said you had no choice – is he blackmailing you over something?"

"Sort of – he said I had to sell drugs for him in order to pay back the debt Liam owed him, and if I refused he would get his men to give me an even bigger beating than what they gave Liam."

"You should have called the police."

"Why? It's not like they were interested in carrying

out a proper investigation into Liam's disappearance, so I believe it would have been a waste of time involving them in something like this."

"Fair point."

"So if you feel the same way, what is the point in you passing on everything I have just told you to the police?"

"Well, I might not bother. I think I might just give Frank Parker another visit."

"Hey, you are not going to tell him I grassed him up, are you? He will kill me!"

"Don't worry, John, I know how to deal with these types of situations. You won't need to worry about Frank Parker anymore."

THIRTY-TWO

JOE GOT OUT OF HIS CAR AND WALKED INTO FRANK Parker's bookies. The same girl as before was behind the counter. After she had finished serving a couple of punters Joe walked up to her.

"Is Frank Parker in?"

"No, he isn't. I am not expecting him to come in today."

"When are you expecting him to come in next?"

"Friday afternoon – although he might not make it in at all. Sometimes, however, he does randomly pop in unannounced. If you need to speak with him urgently he will probably be at the nightclub he owns – Ritzy's."

"OK, thanks."

The woman obviously hadn't recognised Joe from the last time they spoke. He wasn't going to bother going to the nightclub as he very much doubted Frank Parker would be willing to see him after how their previous meeting went. Realistically his best chance to speak with him again would be here walking into his office unannounced, but there was a chance he might be able to follow him if he parked near Ritzy's nightclub and waited for him to leave. Joe decided he would do this. He drove his car in the direction of the nightclub and parked roughly five hundred yards down the road from it, giving himself a view of the front door. This could, of course, be a complete waste of time, as Frank Parker may well not be in the nightclub, and even if he was he might leave via the rear entrance. Joe could well have been using this time to work on his actual paid cases, but he believed he had one last chance to solve Liam Devlin's murder and he believed Frank Parker held the key.

It was Friday afternoon. Joe's stakeout of the nightclub had proved fruitless. He was back outside the bookies; he really hoped Frank Parker was in this time. He walked through the front door and up to the counter. There was a different woman behind it this time.

"Is Frank Parker in?"

"Yes, he is."

"Good, I would like to speak with him, please."

"Who shall I say is looking for him?"

"My name is Joe Wilde – he knows who I am."

"OK, just wait there a minute and I will check if he is free to see you."

Joe watched her exit the counter booth and walk through a door that was beside it. Joe had no intention of waiting for her to come back; after a few seconds he went through the door himself. He saw her in the corridor up ahead just about to knock on a door she was standing beside; she turned to face Joe.

"Er, excuse me, sir, you are not allowed back here – this is for staff only."

Joe didn't respond; he just walked up, pushed her aside and opened the door.

"What the hell? What is the meaning of...? Oh, it's you, Mr Wilde. What an unpleasant surprise."

"Sorry, Mr Parker, he just walked on through here and barged past me. Shall I call the police?"

"No, that won't be necessary, Dawn. Mr Wilde won't be staying long."

Dawn left them and closed the door behind her.

"I really can't think of a reason, Mr Wilde, why you would need to speak with me again. I thought I made it clear during our previous meeting that I do not appreciate people making wild accusations against me and that there was nothing else for us to discuss."

"I would like to talk to you, Mr Parker, about the National League."

"Why on earth would you want to speak to me about the National League?"

"Because you are a member, as well their biggest benefactor."

"Another extremely slanderous accusation, Mr Wilde. You are treading on very thin ice. There is absolutely nothing that links me to that vile organisation. I think it is time you left, otherwise I am going to call the police and make a complaint of harassment against you."

"This is how I think it works, Mr Parker. Since the National League diversified into terrorism they require a lot more funding – funding that you wouldn't be able to provide from the profits of your legitimate businesses alone. So you require other means of income such as dealing in drugs. You have various associates who peddle the drugs for you, then they pass the money raised from the sale of these drugs to members of the National League who spend this money in your bookies. They probably place large bets, although not too large to raise suspicion, on bets with long odds so the chances of a pay-out are negligible. You then pass on some of your increased profits, most likely in cash to the National League."

"You have quite the imagination, Mr Wilde, I must say. Now, it really is time you left. I will give you five seconds and if you haven't left my office in that time I am calling the police."

"It is true, though, isn't it? Go ahead, call them."

"You have no proof of anything you have just accused me of, Mr Wilde."

"Maybe not, Mr Parker, but I would say there is enough circumstantial evidence for the police to start an investigation into you. Then there is always a chance that they will uncover evidence that you are a major dealer and maybe even evidence that links you to the National League. Can you afford to take that risk, Mr Parker? I doubt it would be very good for your business, especially if you were found guilty and had to do quite a lengthy stretch in prison."

"I get the feeling you want something, Mr Wilde, otherwise you would have already contacted the police."

"I want you to tell me everything you know about the National League – in particular any involvement that Liam Devlin and his father had with the National League. If you do that I won't go to the police."

"How can I trust you?"

"You can't, but the way I see it is that you have no choice."

"There is no real connection other than Liam's father was a member of the National League for a while – that is it."

"What about Liam?"

"What about him? He was never a member. The only reason I knew Liam was because he owed me money. I didn't even know that William Devlin was his father until someone in the National League informed me."

"So you never met Liam when his dad was a member?"

"No, I didn't, and I only met his father once – it was in here when he was introduced to me by a National League member."

"Were you aware that Liam was homosexual, Mr Parker?"

"No, I wasn't, Mr Wilde, and forgive my ignorance, but what does Liam's sexuality have to do with me or the National League?"

"Liam told John Wilcox that his first homosexual encounter was at the age of sixteen with a man who was a member of the National League. He didn't say who, though."

"Like I told you, Mr Wilde, I didn't know Liam when he was that age."

"Are you aware of any members of the National League who are gay?"

'There was one that I was aware of, but he is no longer with us.'

"He is no longer a member of the National League?"

"No, I mean he is no longer alive. His name was Robin Griffiths."

"What, the former leader of the National League who was arrested for being the mastermind behind the Westminster bombing that killed Malcolm Walcott and was killed by Islamic converts when in prison on remand?"

"Yes."

"How did you find out he was gay?"

"After he got divorced from his wife he rented the apartment above the bookies for a while. One night I went up to see him to discuss some business. He wouldn't answer when I knocked, but I knew he was in, so I used a master key to let myself in. I heard groans coming from the bedroom, so I went in quietly and had a look. I expected to see him with a woman, but to my surprise he was with another man. He didn't see me and I just left."

"Did you ever confront him about it?"

"No, to be honest, I didn't really care. What he did in private was his own business. I know it wouldn't have gone down well with the majority of the members – they would have been calling for his head. The thing is, he was a great leader and was greatly respected by the members. If it wasn't for him the National League wouldn't be as prominent as it is today. As long as he was discreet then I wasn't going to mention it to anyone; I was happy for him to continue as leader."

"Do you think this is who Liam was referring to when he told John Wilcox about his first sexual encounter?"

"Maybe – Robin was the only member of the National League I was aware was gay, or perhaps he was bisexual – who knows? But there could have been a few others as well. Mr Wilde, you are not the only person who has been in contact with me recently saying they are aware of my affiliation with the National League. A guy came to see me at my nightclub earlier in the week. He said that he and others had proof that I funded the National League and said that if you came round here or the club asking me about my connection with National League and about Liam I was to tell you nothing, otherwise they would give all the evidence they have to the police. I didn't really take him all that seriously, as he wouldn't tell me exactly what proof they had. As you stated you would go to the police if I didn't tell you everything I felt I had little choice but to tell you anyway."

"Who was this man?"

"He didn't give me his name."

"Did he say who 'they' were? As you stated, he said they would give all their evidence to the police."

"No."

"What was this guy like? Could you describe him for me?"

"Sure."

After Frank Parker had given him a description of this man, Joe knew exactly who he was describing; it was DI Whatmore.

THIRTY-THREE

JOE PARKED HIS CAR IN THE DRIVEWAY; HE GOT out, walked up to the front door and rang the doorbell. He only had to wait a few seconds before the door opened.

"Oh, hi, Joe. This is an unexpected surprise – what are you doing here?"

"Oh, you know, I was in the area and I thought I would call in on my mate Phil."

"Would you like a drink of tea or coffee, or maybe something a bit stronger?"

"Alright then, whiskey if you have got any."

"No problem, there is a decanter in my study. I will just be a minute."

"Sure, why don't we just sit in your study?"

"Yeah, OK."

Phil went to the decanter which was sitting on a sideboard; he poured two glasses of whisky, handed one to Joe and sat behind an oak-panelled desk. Joe sat down on a leather chair that was against the wall facing Phil.

"So how is the case going?"

"Which one?"

"You know, the one with the woman who may be selling corporate secrets."

"To be honest, I haven't spent much time on that case recently. I have been more preoccupied with Liam Devlin's murder."

"Why are you wasting your time on it, Joe? You are not even being paid to investigate that case. The police stated it was more than likely a burglary gone wrong, which it probably was."

"Even if it was a burglary gone wrong that doesn't explain the attempt on my life or why Liam faked his suicide to go and live in South America."

"You know Liam's murder and the attempt on your life may not be connected to him fleeing to South America. Maybe he got mixed up in something when he was over there – I mean, he owed money to Frank Parker and various others here, so maybe he ended up owing money to people over there and that's why he was killed. Don't you think it's time you stopped obsessing with this case and got on with your life?"

"On the contrary, Phil, I believe it is all connected and I am now certain who was responsible for Liam's death."

"Who?"

"I don't know the name of the person who killed him – he was just some hired assassin who will probably never be caught – but I know who hired them and the people who tried to kill me: it was MI5, just like that man I met in Manor Park stated it was."

"For crying out loud, Joe, some nutjob spins you a wild conspiracy theory and you lap it up."

"He wasn't some nutjob, though. His name is Alan Watkins and he works for MI5, and what's more, you know him, Phil, don't you?"

"Joe, I don't know what you are talking about. Even if this guy does work for MI5 I have never met him; there are thousands of people employed by MI5 – most of them I have never met and never will."

"He works in counter-terrorism, same as you, Phil."

"Joe, I don't know where you got this information from, but your source, whoever it is, is mistaken."

"I am pretty confident the information I have been given is accurate, as my source is DI Whatmore."

Phil gave a slight laugh. "What, the same DI Whatmore who led a botched investigation into Liam's suspected suicide? Joe, I don't know what it is you are insinuating, but I think you are beginning to lose the plot. I really think you should forget about this case – why not go on a holiday? I think it would do you some good."

Joe reached inside his jacket, removed a gun and pointed it at his friend. "Cut the crap, Phil. If you think that our friendship is going to blind me to what you have been doing you are wrong."

"Joe, what the hell are you doing? Where did you get that gun? Put it away, for Christ's sake, this is madness."

"You know, Phil, there were a couple of things that really bugged me since I met that man in the park whose identity I am now aware of. Firstly the car backfiring that he and even I were convinced at first was a gunshot. It was very convenient that this occurred just before he was going to tell me why MI5 had Liam killed. The other thing that was bugging me was that no sooner had I arrived in Nanawa, surveillance was being carried out on me. You remember when I told you that the guy who tried to kill me in my hotel room in Copacabana was also the tramp who sat outside my hotel in Nanawa from day one? I would say for a surveillance team to be set up that quickly it would have to have been organised before I flew out there, and only Jackie, Sally Devlin and her family knew I was travelling to Nanawa, or so I thought. As for the loud bang we heard in the park: that wasn't a car backfiring; it was indeed a gunshot from a gun that was fired by you, Phil. To be honest, from where you were in the park watching us that was a pretty lousy shot, Phil, to miss him completely."

"It's not what you think, Joe, and anyway, I am not saying anything – not when you have a gun pointing at me and probably some recording device on your person trying to coerce some kind of confession from me."

"I have not got anything on me, Phil." Joe stood up, removed his jacket then emptied out his trouser pockets; he then lifted up his shirt to show Phil he wasn't wearing a wire of some kind. He then put his mobile phone on the desk and chucked his jacket towards Phil. "Here, you can check my jacket pockets as well as the lining of the jacket, and you can check my phone there to make sure it is not recording."

Phil thoroughly checked Joe's jacket and then the phone. "Put the gun away, Joe. It is insulting; we have been friends for nearly twenty years – you are not going to shoot me."

"Well, if you are so confident I am not going to shoot you, then you won't mind if I keep pointing it at you."

"Still makes me nervous, mate. You might fire it accidentally."

"You don't get to call me mate – not anymore, since you were involved in a plot to have me eliminated."

"Joe, if you just leave now I won't involve the police, but if you don't I will use your phone to call the police right now.

Joe remained seated.

"Right, OK, have it your way, Joe."

Phil leant forward to pick up the phone, but just as he was about to pick it up Joe fired the gun and shot him in the hand.

"Arrrrgh, arrgh, what the fuck? You shot me in the hand, you bastard!"

"Phil, I am not leaving here until I get the truth, and unless you tell me everything you will lose more than just your hand – do I make myself clear?"

Phil was groaning in agony; he nodded his head in agreement. Joe got to his feet and walked towards the desk. He picked up Phil's glass, which was now less than half full, went over to the decanter and topped it up.

"Here, have another drink."

"There is a first aid kit in the second drawer down on the right-hand side of the sideboard. There are bandages and painkillers in it – can you get it for me, please? The pain is unbearable. I can't think straight."

Joe edged over towards the sideboard, keeping his gun

trained on Phil; he opened up the drawer and removed the first aid box. He opened it up, removed the bandages and the packet of painkillers, then chucked them onto the desk. He watched Phil remove a couple of painkillers from the pack, wash them down with a swig of whiskey, then start to bandage up his bloodied hand; Joe walked back to the leather sofa and sat down.

"Joe, you seem to be suggesting that I knew in advance that you were flying to Paraguay then travelling on to Nanawa, but if you remember, you only told me about Nanawa when you phoned me when you were already over there."

"Yes, you are right, and I didn't have you down as being involved in this until I realised my office had been bugged. After I spoke with DI Whatmore a few days ago I started to believe that MI5 were the ones behind all this, so I did a sweep of my office, and guess what I found? Two small listening devices – one in my desk lamp and the other in my telephone headset. There may, of course, have been others that I missed. I thought about when they could possibly have been planted and then I remembered that unannounced visit you paid me at my office. I could probably count on one hand the number of times you have actually called in to my office in the past five years, Phil. I also remembered you called just after noon, which is conveniently after Jackie goes out for her lunch, as you were well aware. You knew I would have to go to the kitchen to make the tea, which gave you ample time to place those listening devices."

Phil let out a small sigh in resignation. "When you told me you had been hired by Sally Devlin to investigate

Liam's disappearance as she believed he was still alive I told my superiors. They believed she was just clutching at straws, but they instructed me to get regular updates from you on how your investigation was going anyway, just on the off chance. When you told me you believed the police hadn't been investigating Liam's suspected suicide properly I relayed this back to them and they ordered me to plant listening devices in your office. We learnt from your discussion with Sally Devlin that you had discovered Liam had been researching Asuncion and Nanawa and you were going to fly out there, so we had to have you followed. If Liam was out there we had to find him, so we kept you under surveillance in the hope that you would lead us to him, which you did. We effectively let you do our work for us, and what a brilliant job you did too. You know you are wasted as a PI."

"So who was it you hired to kill Liam and to try and kill me?"

"A group of assassins from different South American countries; we had used them in several operations in the past. They were always very efficient and reliable. However, I doubt we will be using them again after their botched attempt to eliminate you."

"What I don't understand is, why, since I returned to the UK, have you not tried to succeed where they failed and eliminate me?"

"Because after listening in to your conversation with Sally Devlin after you returned we realised that you still had no idea why Liam fled the country; he obviously hadn't told you before we killed him. And you are right – I did know Alan Watkins; he worked in counter-terrorism. I slipped a listening device into your jacket before we went to Manor Park so we could listen to your conversation with this guy if he did actually show up. When the guy sat next to you on the bench I recognised him immediately. When he was about to tell you the reason why Liam was murdered I had to intervene; that's when I fired my gun into the air to scare him off. I was doing it to save your life – if he had told you everything you would have been a dead man."

"I assume Alan Watkins is now a dead man. When I spoke with DI Whatmore he told me that he hadn't heard from his friend in over a week. That's right, Phil, DI Whatmore and Alan Watkins were good friends; before they embarked on their current careers they were previously in the army together. That's why the police didn't look too hard for evidence that suggested Liam's disappearance was anything other than a suicide and suppressed any evidence they – or should I say DI Whatmore – found. This is because Alan Watkins told his good friend that a certain faction within MI5 wanted Liam dead and that he had helped Liam fake his suicide and provided him with a few fake passports so he could start a new life in Paraguay. DI Whatmore did everything he could to keep the truth hidden, and at considerable risk to his career. Alan Watkins didn't tell DI Whatmore why MI5 wanted Liam dead, as he wanted to protect his friend in case MI5 were listening to their conversations."

"Why was he prepared to tell you the truth?"

"To warn me; obviously he knew about the surveillance operation in Nanawa because he was a loyal part of your counter-terrorism branch, or so you thought. Back then even if you did have a suspicion that Liam had been tipped off by an agent in your branch you had no idea it was him. He knew, as you all did, that I was going to keep investigating Liam's murder, and if I kept digging I may well find out the truth and therefore you would have no choice but to kill me. It is also the reason why DI Whatmore recently paid Frank Parker a visit to warn him not to tell me anything otherwise he would be exposed as being the main benefactor of the National League, in case I was able to connect the organisation to Liam. This is all to do with Robin Griffiths, isn't it? You were behind his murder in prison as he needed to be silenced as well. I am guessing he and Liam knew each other and Liam knew what he knew, am I right?"

"You are good, Joe, I have to admit. You are certainly a better detective than you were an agent in MI6. You were always too moralistic and principled to make an effective agent; sometimes we have to do things that may seem extreme and are morally questionable, but we do them for the good of the country."

"Oh, don't give me that 'for the greater good' crap, please."

"Joe, this thing is far bigger than you and me. At the end of the day I am just following orders; I have tried to dissuade you from investigating Liam's murder any further, and more than once I have intervened in order to save your life. Considering how long we have known each other and what we have been through I owed you at least that much, but don't think I would hesitate to kill you now if I got the chance. Malcolm Walcott MP had to be eliminated; if he had gone on to become Prime Minister – which, in all probability, he would have – it would have been disastrous for this country."

"So it was MI5 that was responsible for the bombing, not the National League. It was effectively a state assassination for political gains, even though MI5 is supposed to be politically impartial."

"Don't be so naïve, Joe."

"I doubt this comes from the very highest level of MI5, as that could mean the Home Secretary and possibly even the Prime Minister are complicit in the assassination of Malcolm Walcott."

"Of course not; the director-general of MI5 was blissfully unaware of this operation. This is very much the ideology of an enlightened few within counter-terrorism."

"I am assuming your boss, the director of counter-terrorism Glen Stephens, is one of these enlightened few, or is he blissfully unaware as well?"

"Of course – he was the main driving force behind this initiative."

"Call him now and get him to come round here."

"What?"

"Call him on your mobile and tell him you need to see him as a matter of urgency, as you believe I have uncovered evidence that Alan Watkins was killed by a fellow MI5 agent and I could well go to the national press with the evidence this evening. I would very much like to meet Glen Stephens."

Phil removed his mobile from his trouser pocket and, using his one good hand, speed-dialled his boss then put his phone to his ear.

"If I suspect that you are tipping him off to my presence here I will shoot you in the other hand."

The phone call lasted less than twenty seconds. "He is on his way – should be no more than ten minutes. This is madness, Joe. What do you plan on doing? Kill us? You would never get away with it. Also, without hard evidence of the plot to assassinate Malcolm Walcott, murder Robin Griffiths, Liam Devlin and a fellow MI5 agent, no one will ever believe you – it will just sound like a crazy conspiracy theory. If I were you I would do what Liam did: flee the country and hope that we don't catch up with you."

"Right, listen carefully, Phil. I am going to lock you in this room while I wait in the living room for Glen Stephens to show up; if I hear just one peep out of you when he arrives I will shoot him in the leg and then come in here and shoot you in the head – got it?"

Phil nodded. Joe walked towards the study door, removed the key that was in the keyhole, walked out, closed the door behind him and locked it. He walked to the front door, unlocked it and left it partially open. He then went into the living room, sat down and waited.

THIRTY-FOUR

FIVE MINUTES LATER JOE HEARD A CAR PULL UP outside; he could see the headlights through the net curtains of the living-room window. They went out a few seconds later. Joe got up and hid behind the opened living-room door; a few seconds later he heard a voice.

"Phil? Phil, it's Glen – do you realise your front door is open? Phil, is everything OK?"

Joe could hear him walking slowly towards the living-room door; when he entered Joe stepped quietly out from behind the door, raised his gun and pressed the end of the barrel against the back of Glen Stephens' head.

"What the—"

"No sudden movements, Mr Stephens. Turn around very slowly."

"Joe Wilde, I presume. Where is Phil?"

"He is in his study. Walk slowly towards the study door."

Glen Stephens did as he was told and Joe followed him; when they were at the door Joe moved to the side, keeping his gun trained on him, and unlocked the door. He gestured for him to walk in.

"Phil, you OK? Bloody hell, your hand – what happened to it?"

"He shot me."

"You are in serious shit, Mr Wilde."

"Shut up and sit down, Stephens."

Glen Stephens sat down on the leather sofa Joe had been sitting on; Joe remained standing. He guessed that Glen Stephens was in his fifties but was in good physical shape for his age; his hair was mostly grey with the odd streak of brown. He had an air of arrogance in the way he carried himself. Even though Joe was pointing a gun at him he gave of this aura that he was really the one in control of this situation.

"So he knows everything then, Phil?"

"No, not quite everything, Mr Stephens. Phil told me that MI5 was responsible for killing Malcolm Walcott and he was assassinated for political reasons. I would like to know what those reasons were."

"And if I don't tell you I will end up with a bullet through my hand?"

"Something like that."

"It's OK, Glen, he is not wearing a wire and he gave me his phone and jacket to check."

Glen Stephens nodded to Phil then turned his head to Joe; a slight smile crossed his lips before he spoke. "It's quite simple, Mr Wilde. If Malcolm Walcott had gone on to become Prime Minister of this country it would have set us back decades in the fight against extremist terror, particularly Islamic State. He was in favour of removing the yearly immigration cap that had been introduced last year; he was for reducing the detention time for terror suspects and also reducing prison sentences for those convicted of terror crimes with more emphasis on rehabilitation rather than punishment."

Joe shook his head slightly in disbelief at what Stephens had just told him. "So because you didn't agree with his ideology you made sure he could never become Prime Minister by killing him? Obviously you are not a fan of democracy then, Mr Stephens."

"We did what had to be done, Mr Wilde. Our job of identifying terror suspects and preventing acts of extremist terror is hard enough without some liberal do-gooder who, despite having all the best intentions in the world – making it even harder. Eliminating a member of Her Majesty's government is an extreme measure, but this country's safety is my primary concern, and by doing what we did it has made this country an infinitely safer place."

"I doubt the public would see it that way if they knew that MI5 was going around killing innocent UK citizens."

"The public will never know. We did what had to be done to protect the people of this country – sometimes you have to sacrifice a few to protect the many, and for that reason I do not regret the actions we have taken and can sleep easily at night."

"So where does Liam Devlin come into all of this?"

"We got the National League to carry out the bombing for us."

"What, you just pitched the idea to them and they agreed without hesitation?"

"No, not quite. We only approached one member and that was the leader, Robin Griffiths. We didn't really need to pitch the idea to him as he didn't have much choice."

"You threatened to kill him?"

"No, we had stuff on him. We had carried out surveillance on him and other high-ranking members, as well as planting bugs in their houses. We were looking for any skeletons they may have had in their closets. Let's just say Robin Griffiths had a good few."

"What, his homosexuality?"

"Not just that. Robin Griffiths had a particular type he went for. He liked young men – the younger the better, it seemed. Well, some of them couldn't even be classed as men. We have him on film sleeping with a couple of boys who were under the age of sixteen. Whether he knew they were underage at the time I can't be sure, but it didn't matter; we had all we needed on him. We told him that if he didn't agree to carry out the bombing for us he would be exposed for being a paedophile. All he had to do was propose the plan to his fellow members, obviously leaving out our involvement. In turn for doing this for us we assured him he would not be arrested. We supplied him with the bomb and sent him instructions via text to a burner phone which included when and where to place the bomb, how to set it, and the exact time it was to be detonated."

"I take it Liam and Robin became lovers at some point."

"Yes, it transpires they had sex a couple of times shortly after they first met when Liam was sixteen, but they bumped into each other again by chance at a nightclub a couple of weeks before the bombing and embarked on a relationship. We were keeping Robin Griffiths under surveillance, listening to all his conversations in case he blabbed to anyone that it was actually us that was behind the proposed bomb plot. Very quickly their relationship got more serious. Liam was trying to persuade Robin to turn his back on the National League; they talked about being in love with each other. Robin, it seems, was racked with guilt that he had planted the bomb which killed Malcolm Walcott. One night, a few days after the bombing, they were drinking heavily and they ended up revealing their deepest darkest secrets to each other; that was when Griffiths revealed to Liam that he carried out the bombing for us, as it was MI5 who really wanted Malcolm Walcott dead and told him every detail of the plot."

"It was just two people who really knew the truth – that doesn't strike me as such a big deal."

"The problem is if those two people then start to tell other people and then those people tell others and so on, it can snowball. Robin Griffiths had already told Liam, so we believed there was a high probability he would eventually tell someone else, possibly someone in the National League. If one or two people go to the press and their local MP claiming the secret intelligence service was behind the bombing that killed Malcolm Walcott it would just be dismissed as a wild conspiracy theory. However, if numerous people speak out – especially people who were part of the organisation that planted the bomb – there is more chance prominent people would sit up and take notice, and they could launch an investigation into any possible link."

"So that's why you had Robin Griffiths and Liam Devlin killed. You arranged for Robin to be killed when in prison and hired assassins to kill Liam once I had managed to track him down."

"Correct, for Robin Griffiths we had to make it look like a revenge killing. We gave the police the CCTV footage that showed him and another member of the National League planting the bomb, so they would arrest him for us. We carried out a mock interrogation and he was banged up in HMP Pentonville pending the trial. For obvious reasons he needed to be killed before the trial. We knew there were a few radical Islamic converts in that prison. We approached them via an insider and offered them substantial money, which they would have when released, if they killed Robin. As for Liam, we thought we had got lucky with his suicide, although without a body there was always this nagging doubt he was still alive – which proved to be the case, but all thanks to you, Mr Wilde, we were able to find him."

"I was telling Phil that I had been speaking with DI Whatmore, who had been leading the investigation, such as it was, into Liam's disappearance."

"Yeah, apparently he and that rat Watkins were friends and Watkins tipped him off that we were going to kill Liam," Phil interjected.

"Ah, so that is why the police were saying at the time they were convinced it was a suicide."

"Exactly, and when I last spoke to him I also gave him the clothes and shoes I had been wearing the day I tried to help the victims of the mosque bombing for forensic analysis. I am sure, Glen, that Phil told you I was on the scene shortly after the bomb went off. DI Whatmore requested the forensic testing be expedited as a priority, and do you know what the results showed when they came back? There was not one single trace of blood on my shoes and clothing. Strange, that, considering I touched a couple of the victims and was kneeling in pools of their blood. Yes, the clothes had been thoroughly washed since that day, but even so – not even a single trace. What they did find, however, was traces of corn syrup, trace elements of red, blue and green food colouring, and traces of cocoa powder, coincidentally all the ingredients needed to create realistic fake blood. The way the paramedics arrived so soon on the scene that day just didn't sit right with me, and now I know why. There were no victims of the mosque bombing – just actors playing their part in some elaborate hoax to fool the general public."

Joe believed the way Glen Stephens was now looking at him was with a kind of grudging respect.

"Right again, Mr Wilde. They are called false flag operations. You see, after the bombing that killed Malcolm Walcott we needed to reinforce the narrative that the National League was a significant threat and capable of the most heinous atrocities. They had only ever been responsible for a couple of bombings in their history, neither of which resulted in any deaths, just injuries. For them to all of a sudden target a high-profile

MP and succeed in killing him would seem a bit odd, especially if after this they never again pulled off an act of terrorism that was as devastating and as high-profile. The bomb and the damage to the mosque were genuine, but we made sure that the people we used who were inside were far enough away from that side of the mosque so there wouldn't be any casualties. They would then stumble out the main door doing their dying swan acts. The bomb we used was highly charged but had a very small blast radius. The victims outside the mosque were situated far enough away from it that they wouldn't get caught in the blast but close enough for any witnesses to believe they could sustain minor injuries. It was all choreographed perfectly; we had spent months rehearsing the event."

"I assume all the paramedics and police who arrived on the scene were actually counter-terrorism agents?"

"Yes."

"And who did you use to play the fake Muslim victims?"

"They were informers and assets that we had used in the past. You see, Mr Wilde, false flag operations like this can be very effective in altering the public's perception of certain people and organisations. Through images of the destruction and interviews of mass hysteria and confusion from terrified witnesses, the mainstream media serve as an unquestioning, ultra-effective propaganda vehicle. They effectively act as a brilliant second phase of the false flag operation."

"So you have used them previously in the past?"

"Of course – you think every high-profile act of terrorism, particularly those committed by Islamic extremists you have seen reported, is always genuine?

No, a few in recent years were also false flag operations, like the mosque bombing, and unlike real acts of terrorism, no one gets killed or injured. You see, we are not complete monsters, Mr Wilde."

"That's a matter of opinion."

Glen Stephens began fidgeting like he was starting to become impatient. "Well, as much as I have enjoyed this little chat and helped join the dots for you, Mr Wilde, time is getting on. I would like to know what you intend on doing now you have got all this information from us, because from where I am sitting there is not a lot you can do." The look of self-satisfaction had returned to Glen Stephens' face.

"I could call the police and have you both arrested."

"On what grounds? You have no proof of anything Phil and I have just told you. If anyone is likely to get arrested it is you, seeing as you have shot Phil in the hand and threatened to shoot me. I would say your only option is to try and flee the country before we stop you, and even if you manage that, like Liam, you think we won't be able to find you eventually?"

"That's the thing, though, Mr Stephens, I do have proof. I didn't before our little chat this evening, but I do now." Joe picked his phone up off the desk and started to text.

"I don't understand – what are you doing? Who are you contacting?"

"You remember Mark Thompson, don't you, Phil?"

"Yes, of course. We worked with him for years in MI6 and he helps you out sometimes with your cases. What about him?"

"Well, he has been recording everything that you two have told me this evening."

Phil looked at Joe with a puzzled look on his face then looked at Glen Stephens, who looked at Phil even more puzzled.

"What, how? I checked your phone to make sure it wasn't recording and thoroughly checked your jacket for any listening devices; you also lifted up your shirt to show you weren't wearing a wire."

"Well, you know those two listening devices that I discovered you had planted in my office – where do you think they are now?"

Phil had a look of disbelief on his face. "What, in this room? Bollocks, I have had my eyes on you the whole time we have been in this room together; there is no way you could have planted those without me seeing."

"That's because I didn't plant them this evening. I planted them last night when you were working."

Phil shook his head and smiled. "You are just bullshitting us, Joe. There is no way you could have broken in here last night, and even if you did manage that, you would have triggered the alarm."

"Really? Well, what is that under your desk then?"

Phil, using his uninjured hand, started feeling the underside of his desk. After a few seconds his hitherto smug expression changed. He had felt something; he bent down to look and that's when he saw it: a small listening device was stuck to the underside of his desk. He removed it and held it up. Phil now had an expression of utter disbelief on his face, which then turned to fear.

"Shit, that is why you wanted to sit in here rather than in the living room."

"Yes, as I needed you in close proximity to the bugs. Any time I have been round here you always offer me a drink first; I know where you keep your decanter of Cognac so that is why I requested a whiskey, as I knew you would have to come in here. So I followed you in and suggested we sit in here, as I knew there was a high probability you would say yes just for the sake of convenience. Your living room is much larger, and as I only had two bugs I wouldn't have been able to predict with any certainty where you would sit if we had stayed in there. As for gaining access in the first place, I bought a few different bump keys online, one of which worked on your back door. Mark lent me a wireless burglar alarm jammer and showed me how to use it so I would be able to deactivate your alarm. And guess what else I found when I was in here? This gun. It was in one of the drawers of the sideboard; I might have guessed that a rogue agent would have an unlicensed gun at home. I told DI Whatmore I would text him as soon as I had extracted from you all the information necessary to secure a conviction. He and his team are making their way here as we speak."

"Everything we said to you was clearly under duress; you were pointing a loaded gun at us and you have already shot an unarmed man."

"I think you are clutching at straws there, Glen."

Joe didn't see it coming until it was too late as he was focusing on Glen Stephens. Phil had picked up his glass of whiskey and hurled it towards Joe; it struck him on his forehead and smashed. Joe raised his hands instinctively to his head; as he did Glen Stephens leapt off the sofa, dived towards Joe and rugby tackled him to the ground. He tried to grab the gun out of Joe's hand, but Joe intensified his grip; they wrestled on the ground furiously. While they were struggling on the floor the gun went off. The surprise of the gun going off, coupled with the fact that Stephens had started punching Joe hard in the face with his left hand, meant that he loosened his grip on the gun just enough for Stephens to wrench it free using his right hand. As soon as he had the gun he rolled off to the side and stood up. Joe also got to his feet, but Stephens had the gun pointed straight at his head.

"I am afraid this is the end of the line for you, Mr Wilde."

Joe was expecting the sound of the gun firing to be the last sound he would ever hear, but then he heard a groaning; he and Stephens turned their heads and saw Phil lying on the floor covered in blood, clutching his gut. He got hit when the gun had inadvertently gone off. The next thing Joe heard was a noise coming from the living room, then, suddenly, the study door flew open.

"Police, drop your weapon and slowly get on your hands and knees."

A police SWOT team were aiming their weapons straight at Glen Stephens. He did as he was instructed, and two officers rushed forward and pushed him flat on his stomach; one of them handcuffed him while the other looked over and saw Phil.

"Call an ambulance – we have a critically injured man here."

THIRTY-FIVE

"**Y**OU COULD HAVE BEEN KILLED. I TOLD YOU THAT you shouldn't have confronted them on your own."

Joe and DI Whatmore were sitting in Phil Harkes' living room.

"It was the only way, you know that. They wouldn't have talked otherwise."

"How did you let them disarm you?"

"They took me by surprise – good job you burst in when you did."

"I am glad I insisted we position ourselves in the next street so we were close by; we heard the gunshot when we were running up the garden path. You will need to give a statement regarding what happened in the study. It looks like Stephens is going to claim you shot Phil in the stomach in cold blood before he managed to disarm you."

"That is complete bollocks."

"I know that. The listening devices you planted should have picked up the struggle that ensued before the gun went off. Stephens is going down for a long time; he is just trying to take you down with him as a parting shot. I wouldn't worry too much. I am sure you will be vindicated."

"What about Phil?"

"He was in a bad way when the paramedics took him away as he had lost a lot of blood; it will be touch-and-go whether he makes it. With everything he is facing, especially if it was him that killed Alan Watkins, he would probably rather not pull through. I will need to interrogate Stephens as to how they killed him and where they disposed of his body."

"I am sorry about your friend. If I hadn't have agreed to meet him that day in the park he would probably still be alive today."

"You can't think like that – if you hadn't met him we may not have been able to bring down Glen Stephens and his cabal of rogue agents. Alan died by trying to do the right thing and that is how I will always remember him. I would say it is harder for you, Joe, to accept that your good friend turned into the man he became."

Joe leant forward and stared at the ground for a few seconds while shaking his head slowly. "I had known him for nearly twenty years. He saved my life on more than one occasion when we worked together in MI6. I still can't believe he allowed himself to become embroiled in a state assassination and the killing of innocent men."

"Glen Stephens strikes me as a very charismatic and persuasive man. I would say even stronger-minded men than Phil Harkes have allowed themselves to become brainwashed by his political ideology and views on terrorism. Anyway, I better head back to the station and prepare for my interview with him. I will probably see you around – take care of yourself, Joe."

"Thanks. You too, Detective."

"Please, call me Carl from now on."

Joe contemplated getting up from the armchair he was sitting in to go home; the adrenalin that had been coursing through his body for most of the evening had evaporated and he now felt exhausted.

Just then a heavyset man with thinning brown hair, who was probably around the same age as Glen Stephens, walked into the living room and sat down in the armchair next to Joe.

"Hello, Mr Wilde. My name is Harold Francombe and I am the director-general of MI5. I believe that I and the rest of the service owe you a debt of gratitude. The service has had the odd rotten apple over the years, as you would expect, but a whole branch – that is unprecedented." Harold Francombe paused for a few seconds before he spoke again. "I regret to inform you that Phil Harkes succumbed to his injuries and died in the ambulance before it reached the nearest hospital."

Joe looked at him, emotionless. "He was effectively already dead to me."

"Yes, I can understand why you feel that way."

"You never suspected anything, Mr Francombe?"

"No, nothing – you have to understand, Mr Wilde, that Glen Stephens had been with MI5 for a long time. Right from the very start he was a very effective agent.

He had been involved in foiling some of the worst terror plots ever devised and helped apprehend many notable terror suspects over the years. That bought him a lot of respect and a great deal of trust over the years."

"Sounds like you are making excuses for him."

"Not at all, Mr Wilde, in no way am I making excuses for his actions. What he did was wrong; it was unlawful, immoral and effectively treason. He will quite rightly spend the rest of his life in prison. I am just trying to make you understand that loyalty and trust play a big part in an organisation like MI5, and without it, what have we got? Just take your friend Phil Harkes – you trusted him, didn't you? With your life, I expect. And you were loyal to him, just like you believed he was loyal to you. I don't think you would ever have believed he could get involved in something as corrupt as this. That is the same way I and many others felt about Glen Stephens. Well, thanks to you they and the rest of counter-terrorism can no longer commit such unspeakable crimes. You know, the service could do with someone like you in its ranks. You have a considerable amount of talent, Mr Wilde – and no shortage of experience, I might add, given your previous career with MI6. I would offer you a job; there are certainly plenty of vacancies now in counter-terrorism, but I doubt very much I will be in this job much longer. I am sure I will be forced out."

"Why? You were not involved and you were completely unaware of what Stephens and his section were really up to."

"But I should have been; I am sure that is how the Prime Minister and Home Secretary will see it. The buck stops with the man at the top, as it always does. I will be expected to fall on my sword. I am sure I don't need to tell you this, but I will anyway: the bombing that killed Malcolm Walcott, the false flag operation, the deaths of Liam Devlin, Robin Griffiths and Alan Watkins – the media and the general public must never find out the real truth behind these events. If they did there would be a massive outcry; trust in MI5 – in fact, in all of the secret intelligence service agencies – would hit an all-time low, probably never to recover. The public need to feel safe – these days more than ever – and the best way to help the public remain that way is if they have complete confidence in the secret intelligence service. You should be fully aware of the Official Secrets Act, as you would have signed it when you joined MI6. Do you understand, Mr Wilde?"

"I do, yes."

"Good, and thanks again, Mr Wilde."

With that, Harold Francombe got up and left.

THIRTY-SIX

TWO WEEKS LATER

"YES, NO PROBLEM. SEE YOU ON THURSDAY – BYE."
Joe hung up the phone and picked up the local
newspaper that was on his desk. He didn't often buy the
local rag, but when he popped into the local convenience
store to get a coffee on his way to the office and saw
the headline he had to buy it. He hadn't had a chance
to read the full article yet. The headline stated: "Local
Businessman Arrested on Suspicion of Drug-Dealing."
There was a picture of Frank Parker on the front page in
handcuffs being bundled into the back of a police car. Joe
read the first paragraph:

> *Yesterday afternoon police arrested Frank Parker at his*
> *nightclub on suspicion of drug dealing. The detective*
> *in charge of the investigation, Detective Inspector*

Carl Whatmore, was confident based on the evidence
they had gathered they would be able to bring charges
against Mr Parker, fifty-six.

Joe read on until he got to a bit that stated:

Police started investigating Frank Parker after receiving
evidence from a former drugs pusher who was supplied
drugs by Mr Parker and who sold them on to fellow
students at Walthamstow Forest College. This student
further assisted police by working alongside them until
they had enough evidence that an arrest warrant could
be issued.

It appeared that John Wilcox's conscience had got the
better of him. "Good for him," Joe thought to himself.

Just then Jackie knocked on his door and entered.
"Hi, Joe, just had a call from the CEO of Headstart
Technologies wanting to know if your investigation into
their company employee is nearing its conclusion."

"The investigation is finished, Jackie – I wrapped it up
last night. I will just do up my report and email it to him."

"So you got evidence that she was selling their
company secrets then?"

"No, I didn't, as she wasn't selling their secrets – turns
out her grandfather, who has not long to live, as he has
terminal cancer, gave her fifty thousand pounds in cash
as a gift to avoid inland revenue taking a big chunk in
inheritance tax. He paid her cash because he doesn't
have a bank account as he distrusts the whole financial
banking system."

"Was that Sally Devlin you were on the phone with a few minutes before I came in?"

"It was – we are meeting up for lunch on Thursday."

"Oh, aye," Jackie said with a grin on her face.

"We are just friends, Jackie."

"Of course."

"Anyway, has any work come in?"

"Yes, one – a woman called stating she thinks her husband is having an affair with his secretary and she wants you to follow him. It's just going to be a tedious surveillance job – not very exciting, I am afraid."

Joe smiled. "That's the way I like it."